BEVERLY BARTON

THE REBEL'S RETURN

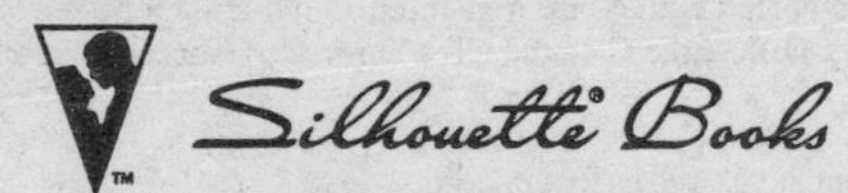

Published by Silhouette Books
America's Publisher of Contemporary Romance

Special thanks and acknowledgment are given to Beverly Barton for her contribution to the LONE STAR COUNTRY CLUB series.

SILHOUETTE BOOKS

ISBN 0-373-61354-7

THE REBEL'S RETURN

This edition published by arrangement with Harlequin Books S.A.

Visit Silhouette at www.eHarlequin.com

Printed in U.S.A.

CLUB TIMES

For Members' Eyes Only

Murder-Mystery Gala Turns Deadly

Last night Maddie Delarue's murder-mystery gala was filled with more drama than a soap opera when the body of Judge Carl Bridges was found floating in the club's front pond! Sources say our very own members were questioned and then released by authorities, but before long, the most likely suspect emerged from the darkness—Dylan Bridges, bad-boy son of Judge Carl who had recently returned to Mission Creek to make amends with dear old dad. If the wealthy stockbroker truly believes an Armani suit can cover up the scoundrel that lies beneath, he's been watching too many *Dallas* reruns. Word has it, though, that Maddie was quick to give Dylan an airtight alibi, claiming she was with him *all night*. It doesn't take a genius to figure out what those two were up to....

On a lighter note, all members will be happy to know that the investigation into the abandoned baby found on the links is making some headway, thanks to P.I. Ben Ashton and his team. And the *Club Times* has also learned that newlyweds Flynt and Josie Carson are about to expand their little family. Talk about some Texas two-stepping!

As always, members, make your best stop of the day right here at the Lone Star Country Club!

About the Author

BEVERLY BARTON

was delighted to take part in the LONE STAR COUNTRY CLUB continuity series and was especially pleased to write *The Rebel's Return* because the bad boy/poor boy and good girl/rich girl theme is one of her favorites. She found it challenging to incorporate characters from other series books into her story and discovered that the residents of Mission Creek, Texas, were quite fascinating. Being able to include a murder mystery in the plot was an added bonus, and turning Dylan and Maddie into multifaceted people with personal histories that bound them together was gratifying indeed.

Award winning, *USA TODAY* bestselling author Beverly Barton is a very happy wife, mother and grandmother, a sixth-generation Alabamian and a proud American, with deep family roots in this country that go back over two centuries.

Welcome to the

Where Texas society reigns supreme—
and appearances are **everything.**

A shocking murder rocks the town of Mission Creek....

Dylan Bridges: When this hard-hearted loner makes a stunning entrance at the LSCC's murder-mystery gala, romance reignites with the woman of his dreams. But an evening of passion is not in the works when a grisly discovery is made and all fingers point to him as his own father's murderer!

Maddie Delarue: This good-girl socialite can't believe her eyes when the roguish rebel from her past strides into the LSCC and boldly sweeps her into his arms for the kiss of a lifetime. Can their newfound love withstand a devastating turn of events?

Mission Creek Musings: What is visibly bereft waitress Daisy Parker doing at Carl Bridges's funeral? Could the real murderer still be at large? And is there any truth to the rumor that missing-in-action international playboy Luke Callaghan could be Baby Lena's proud papa?

THE FAMILIES

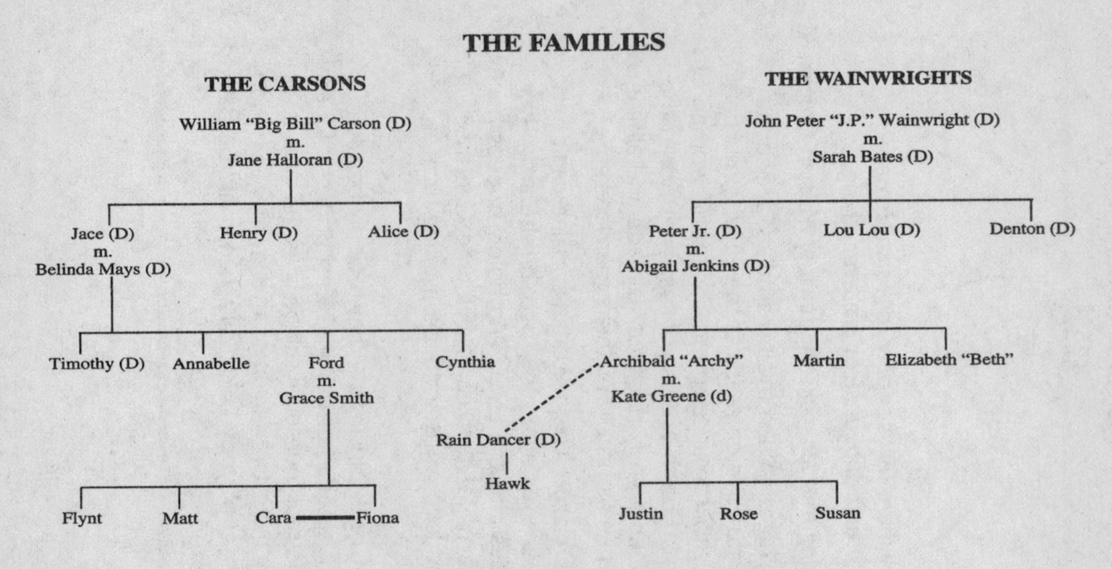

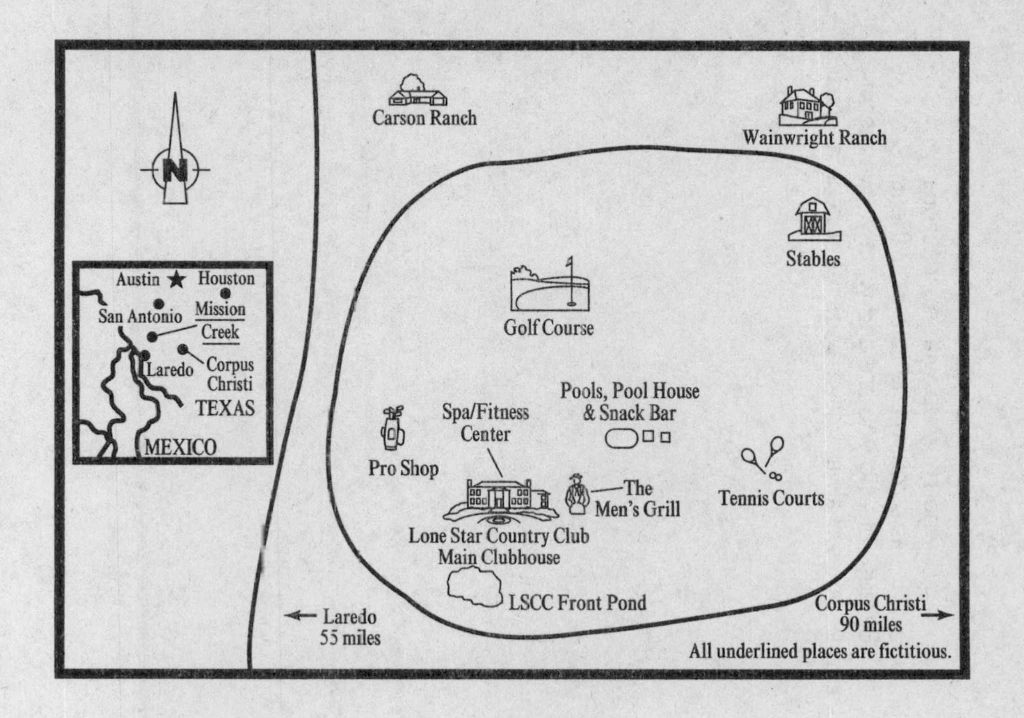
N
Austin
Houston
San Antonio
Mission Creek
Laredo
Corpus Christi
TEXAS
MEXICO
Carson Ranch
Wainwright Ranch
Stables
Golf Course
Pools, Pool House & Snack Bar
Spa/Fitness Center
Pro Shop
The Men's Grill
Tennis Courts
Lone Star Country Club Main Clubhouse
LSCC Front Pond
Laredo 55 miles
Corpus Christi 90 miles
All underlined places are fictitious.

To Melanie Davis Austin,
who grew up with my daughter
as a cousin and as a dear friend.
Because of who you are and what you've meant
to us, you will always have a special place in my heart.

Prologue

Dylan Bridges glared across the courtroom at his father and for one horrific moment felt nothing but hatred for the man. He had kept hoping, up to the very last minute, that his dad would do something—anything—to help him. But the high and mighty, all-important Judge Carl Bridges hadn't lifted a hand—hell, hadn't lifted his damn pinky finger—to help his only child.

Dylan felt like a fool for believing that his father would somehow find a way to stop the inevitable, that he'd pull strings, call in favors or at the very least speak in Dylan's defense. But oh, no, not Carl Bridges, the by-the-book, high-principled, no-excuses lawyer, judge and absentee father. For the past four years, ever since Dylan's mother died, Carl had had no use for him. Leda Bridges had been the buffer between father and son, keeping peace in the family. It seemed to Dylan that once his mother was gone, his father had stopped loving him, and had devoted all his time and attention to his job.

Well, you've had it now, Dylan told himself. *You're on your way to the Texas Reform Center for Boys.*

Two years! He wouldn't be getting out until he turned eighteen. How the hell had this happened to him? He'd done a lot of stupid things in the past few years, even had some skirmishes with the law; but stealing a car had been a major screwup, even for him. A string of misdemeanors was one thing—auto theft was something else entirely.

"I've never been more disappointed by anyone in my entire life," Carl Bridges had said. "Son, what were you thinking? You took that car for a joyride and dragged Jock Delarue's daughter into this mess with you."

Had that been the real problem, the fact that he'd dared to corrupt Mission Creek's reigning princess, Maddie Delarue, whose old man had more money than God? If he had simply borrowed the car from the country club and hadn't whisked Maddie off her feet and practically kidnapped her, would he still be in as much trouble? Probably not. Had his father decided it was easier to betray his son than to displease Jock Delarue? If Dylan knew one thing about his dad, it was the fact that he enjoyed being a golf buddy with the movers and shakers in Texas, especially men like Delarue, Archy Wainwright and Ford Carson.

So, why, of all the girls at Mission Creek High, had Dylan set his sights on Maddie? He'd known she was way out of his league. Was it because the fiery-haired cheerleader was the most popular girl in school? Was it because she represented the unobtainable? Or was it simply because every time he looked at her, he got hard? Whatever the reason, he had become obsessed with the one girl who wouldn't give him the time of day. Other girls found the tough-guy, bad-boy image he'd cultivated intriguing. At sixteen, he was considered the hellion of Mission Creek, Texas—and the bane of his father's existence.

He supposed he could lay all the blame on Maddie; after all, she was the reason he'd taken the sleek silver Porsche that day. Like a fool, he'd been damned and determined to impress her, to show off, to get her alone, even if only for a few minutes. The whole thing had started several months ago, the day he'd finally worked up enough courage to ask Maddie for a date. He had cornered her in the school parking lot that afternoon as she and several of her giggling fellow cheerleaders passed by.

He leaned casually against the hood of his old truck. Unlike a lot of the other guys whose fathers had given them new cars on their sixteenth birthdays, Dylan had been told that if wanted a vehicle, he'd have to work for it. His two part-time jobs—as a weekend valet at the country club and his summer and after-school job at the local hardware store downtown—had earned him just enough money to buy the beat-up, aqua-blue Chevy pickup.

''Hey, Red,'' he called as she walked past him.

Maddie paused momentarily, shook her head just enough to toss about her long red hair, but didn't turn or acknowledge his presence in any way. But her girlfriends turned and looked at him, all smiles and fluttering teenage silliness.

"Look, Maddie, it's Dylan Bridges," one girl said as she curled a lock of her blond hair around her index finger and gave him the once-over.

"Why don't you leave Maddie alone?" Another perky blonde asked. "She's not interested in the likes of you. Why would she want anybody else when she's practically going steady with Jimmy Don Newman?"

Ah, yes, Jimmy Don Newman, a high school senior and captain of the football team. Every girl's dreamboat. Not rich by Wainwright, Carson and Delarue standards, but acceptable because his mother's family had deep roots in Mission Creek and Jimmy Don's athletic prowess had gained him the town's admiration.

"Is that right, Maddie?" Dylan eased away from the truck and took a tentative step toward her. "Do you really agree with all these other airheads who think Jimmy Don's so wonderful? Or are you dying to find out what it would be like between you and me?"

Maddie jerked around and glared at him. "There is no you and me and there never will be."

"Never say never." He winked at her.

She huffed.

When he walked toward Maddie, her friends stepped aside and moved behind her.

"Come on, honey, let me drive you home."

Maddie lifted her chin, stuck out her snooty little nose and glowered at him; then she glanced at his rusty, battered, old truck. "I wouldn't be caught dead in a rattletrap like that. I'd never date a guy who didn't have a decent car."

Her words stung him, but what pissed him off royally was the fact that she stood there so smugly, looking down her nose at him while the tittering laughter of her friends echoed in his ears.

Oh, yeah, he could certainly lay the blame for his present predicament at Maddie Delarue's feet. But his father shared at least half the blame. The very morning he'd borrowed the Porsche from the country club, he and his father had gotten into another rip-roaring argument and he'd stormed out of the house, bitterly angry. Adding to his bad mood when arriving for his valet job at the Lone Star Country Club was Maddie's arrival to play tennis with Jimmy Don. When he saw the two of them together, he'd never wanted anything more in his life than to grab Maddie and run away with her.

And that was just what he'd done.

"That Bridges boy is being sent to the Texas Reform Center for Boys in Amarillo," Jock Delarue said. "It's a damn shame that a fine man like Carl has such a worthless, troublemaking son."

"Perhaps his hoodlum tendencies come from his

mother's side of the family,'' Nadine Delarue commented in her usual superior manner. ''Who was Carl Bridges' wife? I don't think we ever knew her, did we?''

''Can't recall her name.'' Jock laid the *Mission Creek Clarion* aside as he lifted his second cup of coffee. ''I vaguely remember meeting her once. Curvy little blonde. Rather pretty. Didn't we send flowers when she passed away?''

''I'm sure Dodie took care of that.''

Yes, I'm sure Dodie did, Maddie thought. Her daddy's private secretary, Dodie Verity, took care of anything Maddie's mother considered beneath her. Nadine Gibson Delarue didn't bother herself with underlings, except to issue orders or complain about their lack of intelligence or breeding. Her mother had been born in Georgia, the granddaughter of the governor, and once arriving in Mission Creek, Texas, a good twenty years ago, set about procuring herself a position as one of the town's grand dames.

Sometimes Maddie wondered how her cultured, Southern belle mother had ever wound up married to a gruff, plainspoken Texan, who, despite being the richest man in the state, was a down-to-earth, good old boy. Jock Delarue's granddaddy had made a fortune in oil, and his daddy had taken that fortune and tripled it by making smart investments. Maddie sighed. Maybe what she'd heard was true—maybe her mother had married her father for his money.

Growing up, Maddie had basked in her parents' doting love for her and had always been daddy's little girl. Believing herself to be the child of a loving union, she had never questioned the solidity of her parents' marriage. Not until recently. She certainly hadn't seen much affection between the two lately. And even at sixteen, she wasn't totally naive. She'd heard the rumors about her father's other women.

"May I be excused?" Maddie tossed her napkin on the table and scooted back her chair.

"You look a bit pale, dear," her mother said. "Are you upset because your father mentioned that awful Bridges boy? I know how traumatic being kidnapped by that delinquent was for you."

"Hell, Dinie, the boy didn't kidnap Maddie," Jock bellowed. "She told us, she told the police and she testified in court that he didn't force her to go with him."

"I refuse to believe that any daughter of mine would have willingly—"

"Shut up, woman!" Jock looked at Maddie, who stood behind her chair, trembling, tears swimming in her eyes. "You're excused, honey pie."

Maddie nodded, offered her father a weak smile, then ran from the dining room. She didn't stop running until she reached her bedroom, upstairs. And all the while her mind whirled with unanswered questions, with doubts and uncertainties and with an unbidden sympathy for Dylan Bridges.

She tossed herself across her bed and cried as if her heart were breaking. And in all honesty, she wasn't sure her heart wasn't breaking. Her safe, secure and sane life had in a few short months begun to unravel, to come apart at the seams. And there didn't seem to be anything she could do to stop it.

She couldn't help wondering if she was responsible for the constant bickering between her parents; it seemed they seldom had a kind word for each other. When the police had called her parents the day Dylan had taken her for a ride in a stolen car, her mother had blamed her father.

"It's all your fault for allowing her to attend public school and to associate with riffraff," Nadine had said. "If you had listened to me and we'd sent her to private school, she would have known better than to even speak to someone like that Bridges boy."

"My father sent me to public school and it didn't hurt me one bit," Jock had replied. Her mother had simply rolled her eyes. "I felt Maddie needed to learn how to deal with people from all walks of life, just as my father believed that was best for me. Along with great wealth comes great responsibility, you know."

"You should have acted in a more responsible manner toward your daughter!"

Could she have prevented what happened that day? Maddie wondered. Had her comments about Dylan's dilapidated truck a few days earlier prompted him to steal the car that Saturday? Had the embarrassment her mother experienced because of her involvement with Dylan's car theft created a rift between her parents?

Maddie curled into a fetal ball in the middle of her bed and cried until her eyes were red and her nose stuffy. As she uncurled her body, turned over and gazed up at the ceiling, she sniffed several times and wiped her face with her fingertips.

Enough of this feeling sorry for yourself, she thought. Your life hasn't been drastically changed; not the way Dylan Bridges' life has been. He's going away to a correctional facility for underage criminals.

You shouldn't waste your time feeling sorry for him, she told herself. He doesn't mean anything to you.

Was she lying to herself? Was she trying to convince herself that Dylan Bridges had no effect on her whatsoever? If only that were true. She hated the very idea that Mission Creek's rebel without a cause plagued her thoughts day and night. For goodness sakes, she didn't even like him. But she did feel something for him. Those strange, unnerving feelings scared the heck out of her. During the past six months, whenever she saw him, her heart beat a little faster and a her stomach quivered. And heaven help her, she had daydreamed about him kissing her. Her reaction to Dylan was different from anything she'd ever felt. Even when Jimmy Don Newman French-kissed her, she didn't get weak in the knees.

Maddie closed her eyes as memories of that Saturday at the country club six weeks ago flashed through her mind like a movie.

Jimmy Don had picked her up in his red Corvette at ten-thirty for their tennis date. They had played doubles with friends, then eaten lunch at the country club's Yellow Rose Café before Jimmy Don and several of his buddies left the girls alone to go play billiards. Bored with the idle chitchat and endless discussion of next year's Debutante Ball, Maddie wandered around on her own and finally went outside. Looking back at what happened that day, she wasn't a hundred percent sure she hadn't deliberately gone looking for Dylan. But if she had, it had been an unconscious action.

"Hey there, Red." Dylan surveyed her from head to toe. "Looking good today, honey. But then you always look good. Mighty good."

She pretended to ignore him.

"Get tired of Jimmy Don?" he asked.

"No, I did not get tired of— Leave me alone. I don't want to talk to you."

"What would you like to do to me?"

Maddie gasped, understanding the none-too-subtle innuendo.

Dylan laughed. "How about going for a ride with me? It's a beautiful sunny fall day."

"Aren't you working?" She told herself to go back

into the country club, to get as far away from Dylan as possible, but she didn't heed her own warning.

"I get a lunch break," he replied.

"Oh. Well, it doesn't matter because I wouldn't be caught dead in that old truck of yours."

"See that silver Porsche over there?" He pointed to the sleek sports car in the private parking area at the club. "How would you like to take a ride with me in that?"

"But that's not your car."

"It belongs to a friend. He won't mind if I borrow it."

Maddie's moment of indecision obviously prompted Dylan to assume she wouldn't reject his request. By the time she managed to form her thoughts into words, he had raced over to the car, jumped in and started the engine.

Oh, no. Now what? She was not going anywhere with him. Not even in a Porsche. Her mother would be appalled if she ever found out that her daughter had even talked to Dylan Bridges, let alone taken a ride with him.

Dylan eased the car around to the front of the club, flung open the passenger door and grinned at Maddie. "Come on, Red. Live dangerously for once in your life. You know you're dying to come with me."

"I can't."

"Yes, you can."

"No, Dylan, really, I can't. I wish you'd stop pestering me. You get me all confused and I don't like it.''

With that confession, Dylan hopped out of the Porsche, grabbed Maddie's hands and dragged her toward the car. She skidded across the sidewalk, her efforts doing little to halt Dylan's determination. She realized that she really did want to go with him, so her protest was only halfhearted. When they reached the car's passenger side, Maddie jerked her hands back, but Dylan held tight.

''Come on, honey. Don't chicken out on me now.''

''I—I... Oh, all right. But—''

Dylan swept her off her feet. She cried out in surprise, barely able to believe that he'd lifted her up into his arms. He deposited her in the bucket seat, then bolted around the hood and got behind the wheel. As he sped down the circular drive, the wind whipped Maddie's long hair into her face.

I've lost my mind, she thought. A niggling sense of uncertainty fluttered inside her. What was she doing here, flying down the highway with Dylan in a borrowed car?

About fifteen minutes later, Dylan turned off on a bumpy dirt road. After pulling under a tree several yards from the highway, he killed the motor, then threw his arm across the back of Maddie's seat as he leaned toward her. Before she realized his intention, he kissed her. A quick brush of his lips over hers. She gasped.

"What's the matter, honey? You've been kissed before, haven't you?"

"Of course, I've been kissed," she told him. "And much better than that."

Without warning, Dylan grabbed her, lifted her up and over the console and into his lap. She was jammed between the steering wheel and Dylan's lean body. When she felt his erection pressing against her bottom, she panicked and tried to pull free. He manacled her wrists and held both in one hand while he lowered his head and kissed her again. But this time, he took her mouth hungrily, shocking her with the fury of his possession. She trembled. She felt hot. She ached between her thighs. Oh, mercy, this can't be happening.

Maddie knew that she had to stop him now, before he went any further, before she wouldn't have the power to resist. But he kept ravaging her mouth, his tongue seeking entrance. She wriggled and squirmed, but he seemed to enjoy it and moaned into her mouth. She immediately stopped moving. Finally, he lifted his head so that they could both breathe again.

"I didn't tell you that you could kiss me!"

He grinned. A cocky, self-assured smile that created a flurry of butterflies in her belly. "But you wanted me to kiss you, didn't you? You've been wondering what it would be like, the same way I've been wondering."

"No, that's not true, I haven't..."

She looked into his eyes, an earthy moss green, and

recognized a kindred passion unlike anything she'd ever experienced with Jimmy Don or any other boy. Was it possible that he could see the same overwhelming emotion in her eyes?

They stared at each other for an endless moment. Maddie tugged on her bound hands, and he loosened his hold. She lifted her arms up and around his neck, then moved against him, her breasts pressing against his hard chest. When she leaned forward, he watched her, waiting for her to make the next move. She kissed him. Softly. Sweetly. But suddenly that wasn't enough. She wanted more. She wanted a lot more.

Taking charge, Dylan deepened the kiss.

Just as he undid the top two buttons on her blouse and kissed the swell of her breasts spilling over the top of her bra, she heard the sirens. But she disregarded them. By the time she had Dylan's shirt undone and her fingers were caressing his chest, she realized the sirens came from two police cars that were turning off the highway onto the dirt road.

"Damn," Dylan muttered under his breath.

Within minutes two uniformed policemen had parked and were approaching the Porsche.

"What's going on?" she asked Dylan.

"Both of you get out of the car, nice and slow," one of the officers said.

"Dylan?" She stared at him.

"Do what they say, Maddie."

"I don't understand."

"The guy I borrowed this car from must have called the police."

"You *stole* this car?"

"I borrowed it, dammit."

"You stole it!" Maddie flung open the door and got out. Glaring at Dylan, she shouted, "I hate you, Dylan Bridges. Do you hear me? I hate you and I never want to see you again as long as I live."

That had been six weeks ago. Six long, agonizing weeks. Jimmy Don hadn't spoken to her for days afterward. All her girlfriends had asked her a hundred and one questions about Dylan. Her mother had all but disowned her. Only her daddy had comforted her. But she suspected that he'd spoken to Carl Bridges about Dylan. She had wanted to ask her father to intervene on Dylan's behalf—and he could have. With one word from Jock Delarue, Flynt Carson, the owner of the silver Porsche would have dropped the car-theft charges against Dylan. But she didn't dare let anyone, least of all her daddy, know that she cared about Mission Creek's bad boy.

Wasn't it for the best that Dylan was being sent away to Amarillo for two years? At least now she would be safe from him. And safe from her own confusing emotions.

One

Dylan Bridges removed his coat and tie, tossed them on the bed, then slipped out of his Italian loafers and padded across the lush carpet to the closet. He removed a pair of faded jeans from a wooden hanger and retrieved a Texas A&M T-shirt from the top drawer of a built-in dresser. After all these years, he still preferred casual wear to hand-tailored suits and five-hundred-dollar silk ties. He supposed that at heart he was still just a middle-class guy from Mission Creek.

As he changed clothes, he chuckled, thinking about how surprised the good folks in his old hometown would be if they could see him now. Seventeen years ago he'd been shipped off to the Texas Reform Center for Boys in Amarillo, and when he'd walked out of that hellhole after serving his full two years, the last place on earth he'd wanted to go was back to Mission Creek. And the last person he'd wanted to see was his father.

Yeah, his feelings for his old man had only grown more hostile during his incarceration. And even a sweet little letter from Maddie Delarue while he was serving time hadn't lessened his resentment toward her.

Dear Dylan,

I wanted to tell you how sorry I am that you were sent away to reform school. I know I should have tried to help you in some way, but at the time I didn't have the courage to speak to my father on your behalf. Please know that I think about you. Stay strong and keep out of trouble while you're there. I've learned the hard way that life isn't always fair and can throw you some cruel punches.

If you want to write to me, send your letter to the post office box address on the outside of the envelope.

Maddie

Figuring that she'd written the letter either as some do-good, philanthropic club project or simply because she had a guilty conscience, Dylan hadn't responded. And he never received another letter from her. But truth be told, he'd never forgotten Maddie Delarue. In a totally illogical way, she remained the ultimate, unattainable goal.

Dylan made his way into the living room of his luxury penthouse apartment, poured himself a drink—Jack Daniel's, straight—and relaxed in the overstuffed, tan leather easy chair. Why was he thinking about Maddie, a girl he hadn't seen since he was sixteen? It wasn't as if he'd been pining away for her all these years. He hadn't. In his twenties women had come in and out of his life like tourists through a revolving door at a New York hotel. And now, at thirty-three and the wealthiest stockbroker in Dallas, all he had to do was snap his fingers and the lovely ladies came running.

The only reason he'd thought about Maddie was that he planned to return to Mission Creek. He was going to do something he'd thought he would never do—go home to see his father. And who knew, he'd probably run into Maddie while he was there. Maybe he'd make a point of it.

Nothing would please him more than to show her—and everybody in Mission Creek—that the town bad boy had turned out all right. Actually better than all right.

After leaving Amarillo, he'd bummed around the country for a couple of years, had attended some night classes at several community colleges and then had come home to Texas and settled in Dallas. The odd thing was that when he finally channeled his energy—including his anger and aggression—into something productive, he discovered he had a talent for finances, the stock market in particular.

The kid who'd been sent to reform school for stealing another man's Porsche now owned one of his own. And a Jag and several antique vehicles. His penthouse apartment had cost him in the millions, he owned a home in Aspen and he was part-owner of a chain of resort hotels in the Bahamas.

Oh, yeah, a part of him would love to rub Maddie Delarue's nose in his success. Of all the people back home, she was the only one he really wanted to impress. She was probably married now, with a couple of kids. Surely she hadn't married Jimmy Don Newman, Dylan thought.

Since her father's death a few years ago, she was now the richest woman in Texas. Dylan chuckled. Hell, maybe she wouldn't be that impressed with him after all.

Grinning, Dylan sipped on his whisky. Even after several days of mulling over the entire matter, he still found it difficult to believe that his father had called him. Out of the blue, after all this time, Judge Carl Bridges had set aside his unswerving pride and telephoned his only child.

"Son, I'm asking you to forgive me," Carl had said. "Can you find it in your heart to give your father a second chance? Is there any hope that we can put the past behind us and build a new relationship?"

Strange that he hadn't vented years of frustration and rage directly at his father. Even stranger was the fact that he, too, wanted nothing more than to put the past to rest, to reach out and forge a new relationship with his father. As a man of experience, he now realized what a rebellious hellion he'd been as a teenager, and how both he and his father had allowed their grief over Leda Bridges' death to separate them instead of bring them closer together. Yes, his father had made mistakes, had concentrated on his career more than his son, had given Dylan no room for failure. But Dylan knew that he had made a lot of mistakes himself, that he'd acted up time and again hoping to get his father's attention.

If staunch, unyielding Carl Bridges could admit mistakes and ask for forgiveness, then so could his son.

Dylan had ended his conversation with his father by saying, "Yeah, Dad, I'll think about coming to Mission Creek for a visit. I just need some time to get used to the idea."

This morning when he awoke, he decided right then, even before his first cup of coffee, that there was no better time than the present to find out if his dad and he could reconnect as father and son. Besides, he needed a vacation. He worked too much; even his closest friends told him he'd become a workaholic. But despite his wealth and great success, he didn't have anything else in his life that truly mattered. Only work.

Long ago, he'd come to the conclusion that a guy couldn't count on anyone or anything except himself. Family was a bogus term. He felt as if he'd lost his only family when his mother died. The desire to marry and start a family of his own had eluded him, mainly because he'd never met a woman he thought he could spend the rest of his life with—never loved or trusted a woman enough to make a serious commitment.

He supposed he should call his father and apprise him of his plans, but he liked the idea of just showing up on his dad's doorstep and surprising him. He'd already gotten a reservation on a flight to Mission Ridge, the nearest airport to his hometown. He'd be home in time for supper. Maybe he'd take his dad to the country club, to the Empire Room. Now, wouldn't that be something—to go back to the Lone Star Country Club as a guest instead of an employee.

And who knew, maybe if things worked out with his father, he might even relocate to Mission Creek.

"Mrs. Delarue, please stop." Alicia Lewis jumped up from behind her desk in Maddie Delarue's private office space in the Lone Star Country Club and rushed forward toward her boss's mother. "Maddie is very busy and I'm not supposed to let anyone disturb her."

"Well, my dear young woman, I'm Maddie's mother and I can assure you that I'm not just anyone." Over the years Nadine Delarue had perfected the royal put-down. "My daughter's position as the events manager here at the club is nothing more than a hobby for her anyway, so she can't possibly be that busy."

Hearing the ruckus outside her office, Maddie groaned. Oh, Lord, just what she needed this afternoon—dealing with her self-pitying, hypochondriacal mother. For the past sixteen years, ever since her parents' widely publicized, bloody divorce and her father's death a few years back, Nadine had clung to Maddie with a tenacious stranglehold. Only by sheer force of will had Maddie been able to live her own life. But her life was often interrupted by her mother's histrionics. Maddie did her best to be the dutiful daughter, but there were times when the burden became almost too much for her to bear.

When Maddie opened the office door, she found Alicia standing there blocking Nadine's path. The moment her mother saw her, she burst into tears.

"This awful girl wouldn't let me see you." Nadine hiccuped. "And I told her that I was your mother."

Oh, great, her mother was tipsy. "It's all right, Alicia." Maddie patted her assistant's shoulder. Alicia was new on the job, so this was her first encounter with Nadine the Terminator. When the bewildered young brunette stepped aside, Nadine flung herself at Maddie, who wrapped her arm around her mother's shoulders and led her into her office. "Have you had anything to eat today? You seem a little unsteady."

As Maddie closed her office door, her mother wiped her eyes and sniffed several times. "I had lunch with the girls here at the club," Nadine said.

"I see." Lunch had undoubtedly consisted of several martinis. "I don't mean to rush you, Mother, but I am very busy this afternoon. The Mystery Gala at the club is this weekend and I have a zillion loose ends to tie up. Is this something that could wait?''

Nadine slumped down on the sofa, upholstered in a beige-and-white striped silk. Maddie groaned internally. No way was Nadine going to let her get off so easily.

''You're always too busy for me.''

Nadine stroked the soft waves of fine white-blond hair that lay close to her face in an attractive, modern style that her hairdresser had assured her took years off her appearance. But not nearly as many years as her most recent facelift, Maddie thought. Since the day her husband had walked out on her, left her for a much younger woman, Nadine had been obsessed with staying young. After the divorce, she'd gone through a succession of suitors half her age, but was left high and dry by each one when they realized that her divorce from billionaire Jock Delarue had not gained her half his net worth. Grandfather Delarue had been a smart old buzzard; he'd insisted Nadine sign a prenuptial agreement before she wed his only son, something not standard procedure in the mid-sixties.

''I'm sorry, Mother. Really I am. But I do have a job, you know. Responsibilities. People counting on me.'' Maddie eased her behind down on the edge of her elaborately carved, antique mahogany desk.

''I'm counting on you, Maddie. You're all I have in this world.''

Oh, here we go again, Maddie thought. I'm all

alone. No one needs me. No one loves me. I gave birth to you. An excruciating labor. You were a colicky baby. My every thought since the day you were born has been of you. She'd heard it all before—ad nauseam.

"What do you want? What can I do for you today?" Maddie focused her attention directly on her mother.

"I—I...well, I'm not sure. It's just that the others, my friends...well, they were all going home to husbands. And you know that I don't have a man in my life. And they all have grandchildren to dote on. I'd think the least you could do is give me a grandchild."

"I'd like nothing better, and maybe someday I'll—"

"Why must you work here? Why do you bother with such a mundane little job? You're the wealthiest woman in Texas. For God's sakes, Maddie, your father left you several billion dollars. You don't need to work. If you spent half as much time socializing as you do playing with this silly job of yours, you might find a husband."

Maddie groaned. Nadine hiccuped, then shook her head, as if trying to clear the cobwebs.

"I socialize," Maddie said. "But let's face it, I haven't had much luck with men. They all seem far more interested in my money than in me. Does that ring a bell, Mother?"

"No need for you to be cruel. And there's no need

for you to remain single, either. There are several eligible men in Mission Creek. Young men wealthy in their own right. You could have had Flynt Carson or Matt Carson if you hadn't let them get snapped up by other women. Neither of whom was half as suitable as you to become a Carson bride.''

''Let's don't go there again. I've known Matt and Flynt all my life. They're simply my friends. They could never have been anything more.''

Tears trickled down Nadine's rosy cheeks. She sniffed several times. ''Why must you scream at me? I'm not a well woman.'' She clutched her silk blouse where the material draped across her breasts. ''Sometimes I don't know why the good Lord sees fit to let me go on living. I suppose I haven't suffered enough.''

Nadine stood on wobbly legs and made a valiant—if somewhat overly dramatic—effort to walk toward the door. Halfway there, she stumbled. Maddie rushed to her mother's side, slid her arm around Nadine's waist and sighed deeply.

''Let me drive you home,'' Maddie said. ''A nice, long drive in the fresh air will be good for both of us.''

''Yes, dear, that would be lovely.'' Nadine patted Maddie's cheek. ''You can be such a good daughter…when you want to be.''

Maddie sat her mother back on the sofa until she could clear off her desk and retrieve her handbag. On the way out, she instructed Alicia to forward any important calls to her cell phone and take messages about anything that could be handled tomorrow.

Ten minutes later, with Nadine secured by the seat belt in Maddie's white Mercedes-Benz convertible, they headed down Gulf Road, past County General Hospital. With wind humming around her, her hair flying like a bright red flag, Maddie shut out the sound of her mother's droning whine. Complain, complain, complain. Was there never any end to it? Why couldn't her mother be content? Sometimes Nadine didn't care that no one responded to her incessant chatter; all she seemed to require was an audience to listen.

Still tuned out to everything except her private thoughts about the upcoming gala at the club, Maddie whipped the convertible off the road and into her mother's private drive. After their divorce, Jock had generously given Nadine the home they had shared for nearly twenty years, and Maddie now paid for the upkeep as her father had once done. The palatial Georgian sat on twenty acres, all immaculately groomed.

Maddie parked, helped Nadine from the car and to the front door. Instead of bothering with trying to unlock the door, she simply rang the bell. Ernesta Sanchez, her mother's longtime housekeeper, opened the door.

"Oh, my, Señora Delarue, are you all right?" The short, squat Ernesta's concern was genuine. Maddie knew, even though her mother would never admit being fond of a servant, that Ernesta was probably her mother's best friend.

"Mother's had a busy day." Maddie escorted Nadine past Ernesta and into the huge marble-floored foyer. "She had lunch with the girls at the club." Maddie and Ernesta exchanged so-she-had-too-much-to-drink glances. "I'll have one of the valets bring her car home later. She didn't feel quite up to driving herself."

"Let me help you." Ernesta took Nadine over completely, her big arm securely circling her employer's waist. "What you need is a nice, long afternoon nap."

"Yes, you're probably right," Nadine said, smiling forlornly at her housekeeper. "I am a bit tired." Nadine glanced at Maddie. "Do you mind terribly, dear? I'm sure you'd hoped we could spend the afternoon together. But I'm afraid I suddenly have a horrific headache."

"I don't mind," Maddie said. "Let Ernesta help you up to your room. I'll run along, but I'll phone later this evening to check on you."

"Yes, do that. Please. I do so look forward to your calls." Nadine allowed Ernesta to lead her toward the massive staircase. "You should phone more often. I get terribly lonely."

"I promise that I'll do better in the future."

While Nadine leaned on Ernesta as the two walked up the stairs, Maddie let herself out and rushed to her car. She sat behind the wheel for a couple of minutes, contemplating her mother's life and their relationship. She had been trying—unsuccessfully—for the past ten years to get her mother to see a psychiatrist, to seek professional help for her depression, but Nadine adamantly refused.

"I'm perfectly sane," she'd said. "As sane as any woman could be whose husband humiliated her in front of the whole world. The man promised to love and honor me, to be faithful to me until death. Whatever you do, Maddie, never trust any man. They're all alike. They'll break your heart."

Snap out of it, Maddie told herself. If you let yourself, you could wallow so deeply in your mother's self-pity that you might wind up drowning in it the way she has.

Twenty minutes later, Maddie parked in the garage in the basement of her condo. After college, her mother had insisted she move home with her, but Maddie had struck a blow for independence then and there. And she'd never regretted having moved into the condo and separating herself from her mother. If she hadn't done that, she doubted she would have survived without psychiatric help of her own.

As she unlocked the door of her three-thousand-square-foot, two-story home, she heard music playing. That could mean only one thing. Thelma was here. Thelma Hewitt was her personal maid, a five-foot-tall ball of fire, with gray-streaked, short black hair and keen brown eyes that saw straight through most people and especially Maddie. Highly efficient, but a notorious busybody, Thelma had worked for Maddie for twelve years. Maddie hadn't wanted a live-in maid, having grown up with a house full of servants. Being a daily maid had suited Thelma just fine. After all, she needed time for her husband, five children and fifteen grandchildren.

After tossing her handbag and keys on the velvet Louis XIV chair in the foyer, Maddie followed the sound of the country-western music, which led her into the kitchen. There stood Thelma, singing along with an old Eddy Arnold tune, peeling apples and dropping the slices directly into an uncooked pie shell.

"You look busy," Maddie said.

Thelma gasped, dropped her knife and the half-peeled apple onto the granite countertop. "Good Lord, gal, you scared the bejesus out of me!"

"Sorry, I thought you heard me walk in."

Thelma wiped her hands on her apron, reached over to turn off the radio, then looked Maddie up and down. "What are you doing home at three o'clock?"

Maddie eased up and onto a stool at the bar area that ran behind the work center. "I had to drive Mother home from the club."

Thelma raised her eyebrows. "How is Nadine?"

"The same."

"Are you okay?"

"Sure, I'm fine." Thelma was a mother-to-the-world type of woman and she'd been mothering Maddie since the first day she came to work for her. "I just wish there was something I could do for Mother, some way I could help her."

"Nadine doesn't want to be helped. She wants to be pitied. So you just go on pitying her and doing what you can. Can't nobody help that woman but herself. You should be concentrating on your own life a bit more."

"Is this the get-married-and-have-babies talk that we've had on numerous occasions?"

Thelma picked up the apple and the paring knife. "I know you modern girls think you don't need a man to complete your life or kids of your own to give you a reason to live, but—"

"But you think I'm the kind of woman who needs to have a husband and children." Maddie reached over and picked up an apple slice from inside the pie pan. "On that one subject, you and Mother agree totally." Maddie popped the apple bite into her mouth.

"There's a man out there waiting for you. You just haven't found him yet."

"There are dozens of men out there waiting for me," Maddie said. "Probably hundreds, if not thousands. And they all want one thing—my money. You know the funny thing is that Mother wants me to get married and give her grandchildren, but at the same time she warns me to never trust any man. And you know what, Thelma? I don't trust men. Not any of them."

"Ah, but one of these days—"

"One of these days, what? Some daring man will sweep me off my feet, make mad, passionate love to me and not give a damn that I'm the richest woman in Texas?"

"Something like that."

"You're daydreaming."

"Dreams are free, Maddie, my girl. If we don't have our dreams, we don't have anything. So what's wrong with your dreaming about being swept off your feet by some handsome man?"

"The last time I got swept off my feet, I wound up at the police station. It seems my Romeo had stolen a car to impress me."

"You're talking about that Bridges boy...Dylan Bridges. That youngun sure was a boil on his daddy's backside. Did everything and anything to rile the judge. I wonder whatever happened to him. Last time I saw him was right before he got sent off to Amarillo to that reform school. Lord, he was a sight, with that long hair and that earring. Looked like a damn hippie."

Maddie hopped off the stool, opened the refrigerator, removed a bottle of Perrier and headed for the door. "I think I'll get some work done in my study. Say goodbye before you leave, okay?"

"Sure thing. And I'll bring you a piece of this pie, just as soon as I take it out of the oven."

Maddie smiled, then escaped to her study, a small, cozy retreat, with floor-to-ceiling bookshelves on three sides and a wall of windows on the fourth. As she positioned herself in the oversized, navy-blue leather chair and placed her feet on the matching ottoman, she thought about Dylan Bridges. Over the years she'd thought of him from time to time, and always wondered what had happened to him. Rumors had abounded: he'd become everything from a mercenary to a priest. Which was highly unlikely because his family wasn't Catholic.

Where was Dylan now? And what was he doing? He'd been one boy who hadn't given a damn that her daddy was Jock Delarue. He'd liked her. Wanted her. She'd known that fact as surely as she'd ever known anything. If only Dylan had come into her life later, when she'd been more mature—when they'd both been adults.

If she met a guy like Dylan Bridges now, would she have the guts to reach out and grab him? Or would she let her doubts and insecurities about love, marriage and men in general stop her from taking a chance?

Maddie shrugged. What difference did it make what she might or might not do? She was about as likely to meet a man like Dylan Bridges as she was to sprout wings and fly.

Two

For just a split second Dylan felt as if he'd stepped back in time. Seventeen years. The old home looked the same, there on the big, level lot in the middle of town, only a few blocks from the courthouse. Did his father still walk to work every morning and then home again in the evenings? Probably. Carl Bridges was a creature of habit. If other things had changed about him, that probably hadn't.

His father had inherited this 1920s Craftsman style house from his uncle, who'd died a bachelor. Like many of the homes of its day, the Bridges house possessed two stories, a sloping roof line, a large square front porch with a swing and a detached two-car garage. The white picket fence around the property boasted a fresh coat of paint, as did the house. Dylan wondered if his great-uncle's old Packard was still parked inside the garage. As a teenager, he had longed to get behind the wheel of that antique gem, but his father had refused to let him even sit inside the car.

A large American flag, waving slightly in the wind, hung over the porch. His father, a Vietnam veteran, had been, in the best of times, a patriotic citizen, and no doubt he was now more so than ever. Looking back to his boyhood, Dylan could recall many reasons to have been proud of his dad. Why couldn't he have realized it at the time?

As he stepped away from the cab and onto the walkway that led up to the front porch, Dylan experienced a moment of uncertainty. Standing at the front door, he hesitated before ringing the bell. Maybe he should have telephoned first to tell his father he was coming. Why the hell had he wanted his arrival to be a surprise?

Reminding himself that his father had been the one to call him, to extend the olive branch, to ask forgiveness, he punched the doorbell. Within seconds he heard footsteps inside the house, then the front door opened and there stood a broad-shouldered, stern-faced man of sixty, with a stock of neatly trimmed white hair and the same watery-blue eyes that Dylan remembered so well.

A sudden smile flashed across Carl Bridges' face as he reached out to grab Dylan's arm. "Come on in, son. Come on in." Carl draped one arm around Dylan's shoulders and escorted him into the house.

Dylan wasn't sure what he had expected. A cordial handshake at most. But certainly not this warm, enthusiastic welcome. His father had never been an overly emotional man, and never one for displays of affection. The only hugs and kisses Dylan had gotten as a boy had come from his gentle, loving mother.

‘‘I had no idea you would come home so soon,’’ Carl said as he led Dylan into living room. ‘‘I’d hoped you would want to see me as much I wanted to see you, but…’’ Carl cleared his throat.

Dylan stared at his dad, startled by the fact that the old man was almost in tears. This wasn’t the Carl Bridges he remembered. And this softer side of his father unnerved him. He had been prepared for both of them to feel and act a bit awkward, but it had never entered his mind that his father might have mellowed with age.

‘‘Have you had supper?’’ Carl asked. ‘‘I could make us some sandwiches here at the house. Or if you’d like we could run over to the Mission Creek Café for some barbecue. Whatever you’d like.’’

‘‘Sandwiches here are fine with me, Dad.’’ Odd how easily he could say that word. Dad. And even more strange was how comfortable he felt in this house. The place had never felt more like home than it did at this very minute.

Dylan glanced around the living room and found fresh tan paint on the walls and a new sofa and chair. The same simple wood paneling around the fireplace and the sturdy coffee and end tables remained, but wooden shutters had replaced the heavy curtains and window shades.

‘‘Come on back into the kitchen with me, son, and let’s talk.’’ Carl nodded the direction. ‘‘I’ll fix ham and cheese. That used to be your favorite.’’

His dad actually remembered what his favorite sandwich had been. He would have sworn that his father hadn't known a thing about him back then, certainly nothing as personal as his preferences in food. Guess it just went to show how wrong he'd probably been about other things, too.

"Yeah, it's still my favorite." Dylan followed his dad into the kitchen, a room that had changed even less than the living room. A new refrigerator seemed to be the only major difference. And the walls were now beige instead of the sunny yellow his mom had painted them.

"Sit down. Sit down." Carl opened the fridge and began removing items, laying ham and various condiments on the table. "Tell me about yourself, Dylan. I know you live in Dallas and that you're a stockbroker. That private detective I hired to find you told me that much."

Dylan pulled out one of the wooden ladder-back chairs from the table and sat. "Why did you hire a private detective? Why didn't you just use your local and state law enforcement connections?"

"You know me, boy, I go strictly by the book whenever possible. I call in favors only if I have no other choice." Carl sliced several thick slabs of ham. "There are times when a man gets himself in a jam and he has to do whatever is necessary to get himself out of trouble."

Staring at his father, Dylan wondered if he'd heard

him right. "Are you in some sort of trouble? Is that why you asked me to come home? Do you need my help?"

Carl took a loaf of bread out of the cupboard, removed four pieces and placed them on two earthenware dinner plates. "I asked you to come home because I want a chance to get to know my grown son and—" Carl cleared his throat "—to make amends for past mistakes."

"You weren't the only one who made mistakes," Dylan said. "I wasn't blameless. I screwed up a lot, and most of the time it was on purpose. It seemed to be the only way I could get your attention."

"I'm not making any excuses, but...well, I had a mighty difficult time after your mama died." Carl spread mayonnaise and hot mustard on the bread, then stacked ham, cheese, lettuce, tomatoes and dill pickle slices before adding the top piece of bread. "I should have been a better father. I should have done something to help you after you stole that Porsche from the country club. I let my stupid pride keep me from doing what I really wanted to do. But at the time, I told myself I was doing the right thing, letting you learn your lesson the hard way."

"That's exactly what I did," Dylan said. "I had to learn everything the hard way back then. Even when I left the reform center, it took me a few more years to get on track and turn my life around."

"You've done well, son, and I'm awfully proud of you."

Dylan swallowed hard. "I...uh...I thought about calling you, you know. Over the years. From time to time. I even considered coming home, but I always chickened out. I wasn't sure you ever wanted to see me again."

Carl placed the plate in front of Dylan, walked around the table and laid his hand on Dylan's shoulder. "Not a day has gone by since you left for Amarillo that I haven't thought about you, worried about you and...cared about you."

Dylan clenched his teeth, then lifted his hand and laid it on top of his father's. "We've got a lot of catching up to do. That's why I've come home for a while."

Tears misted Carl's eyes. "Thank you, son. Thank you."

While nibbling on a Caesar salad, served to her at an umbrella-shaded table on the patio adjacent to the club's outdoor swimming pool, Maddie went over her checklist for the Mystery Gala coming up in only a few more days. Everything was set. The menu had been approved by Chef Tomas. The jazz band from New Orleans was due to fly in on a charter plane on Friday afternoon at one. Actors from the local Little Theater had been hired to play the murder victim and the police detective, and both had been sworn to secrecy on the mystery plot. Mrs. McKenzie, the talented designer who owned Mission Creek Creations, had whipped up a perfectly divine little black satin gown for Maddie, and a matching satin shawl with pearls and Austrian crystals dripping from the edges. She'd wear diamond earrings and a couple of her diamond bracelets, but no necklace. Understated elegance was the style she preferred.

One of the things Maddie enjoyed most about being filthy rich was being able to afford the best clothes money could buy. Some people called her a clotheshorse; maybe she was. Well, actually, no maybe about it. Her walk-in, fourteen-by-sixteen closet was a dead giveaway.

A young waitress who was part of the staff that rotated shifts in the Empire Room, the Yellow Rose Café and the temporary Men's Grill replenished Maddie's iced tea, then asked, "Would you care for dessert today, Ms. Delarue?"

"I'm not sure." What was the young woman's name? Maddie tried to remember. Daisy something or other, wasn't it? "Maybe some fruit. Let me think a minute, please…Daisy."

The waitress smiled. Ah, Maddie thought, I must have gotten her name right.

Wearing a modest one-piece dark green bathing suit, Josie Carson stopped by Maddie's table on her way to the pool. "Working hard, I see."

''Just going over things for the Mystery Gala Friday night. You and Flynt are coming, aren't you?''

''We wouldn't miss it.'' Josie smiled, her face alight with a surreal glow. ''Unless I have another serious bout of nausea and wind up in bed again.''

''Nausea? Have you been sick?'' Maddie asked, thinking the young bride looked the very picture of health.

Josie laughed. ''I'm not sick. Not the way you think. I'm pregnant.''

''Oh, Josie, how wonderful!'' Maddie shot up out of her chair and hugged Josie. ''Flynt must be ecstatic.''

''He's so attentive that he's driving me crazy.'' Josie's emerald eyes sparkled. ''You'd think no other woman had ever had a baby.''

''The man's madly in love with you, so just relax and let him pamper you. That's what prospective fathers are supposed to do. Right?''

''I guess so. By the way he acts with Lena, he's already shown me what a wonderful father he's going to be.''

''How is little Lena?''

''Growing bigger and prettier every day.''

''I don't suppose there's any news about her real parents?''

Josie shook her head, swinging her shoulder-length, platinum-blond hair about her face. ''I'm really torn about Lena. I know it's selfish of me to want to keep her. Flynt and I adore her so much. But somewhere out there she has a mother, possibly both parents.''

Maddie suddenly remembered the waitress who stood attentively waiting for her to decide about dessert. ''Oh, Daisy, I'm sorry to have kept you waiting. I'd like a bowl of strawberries. No cream.''

''Yes, ma'am.'' Daisy turned to Josie. ''Mrs. Carson, may I add my congratulations about your pregnancy? This must be a wonderful time for you and your husband. And I imagine having a child of your own will help y'all give up little Lena when...if her real mother shows up to claim her.''

''Thank you, Miss...Daisy, is it?'' Josie smiled at the young waitress.

''Yes, ma'am. Daisy Parker.'' Daisy turned her attention to Maddie. ''I'll bring those strawberries right back out, Ms. Delarue.''

''Thank you,'' Maddie said, then when Daisy hurried off, Maddie hugged Josie again. ''Give Flynt my love and tell him how happy I am for the two of you.''

Josie nodded, then headed toward the pool. Maddie slumped down in her chair and glared sightlessly at her planning book lying open on the table. Josie Carson was pregnant. How did it feel, Maddie wondered, to be carrying the child of the man you loved—a man who adored you. She'd probably never know. Not all of her billions, not even all the money in the world, could buy her the kind of happiness Josie and Flynt shared.

Dylan and Carl sat up until nearly midnight. Father and son talked—really talked—for the first time in

Dylan's life. They reminisced about the years before Dylan's mother died, when they had been a family. Then they caught up on the years they'd lost during Dylan's self-imposed exile, each cautiously sidestepping any discussion of the events directly prior to and following Dylan's two-year term in the Reform Center. Twice during the evening, Carl had received phone calls that obviously upset him, but he assured Dylan that it wasn't anything to worry about, simply legal matters that he was having a slight problem solving. And since he was just getting reacquainted with his father, Dylan didn't press Carl to disclose the particulars.

As the evening wore on, they shared a pot of coffee and kept talking. Carl wanted to know everything about Dylan, all the details of the years they had spent apart. And Dylan found himself questioning his father about Mission Creek and some of the people he remembered from his youth.

"So, whatever happened to Maddie Delarue?" Dylan asked.

Carl sighed. "Jock's dead, you know. Died a few years back."

"Yeah, I'd heard. When a man as important as Jock Delarue dies, the whole state knows about it."

"Maddie inherited everything, except for some sizable charitable donations and the trust fund he'd set up for his second wife, Renee," Carl said. "You know he divorced Nadine and married a girl not ten years older than Maddie, whom he'd been having an affair with for years.''

''When did that happen? The divorce?''

''Oh, about a year after...'' Carl paused, then looked Dylan square in the eyes. ''You were still in the Reform Center, so I suppose Maddie was seventeen.''

Seventeen? He'd been seventeen when he'd received that strange letter from Maddie, the one telling him that life could throw you some cruel punches. Hell, she'd probably written to him around the time of her parents' divorce. Back then, he'd been too self-absorbed to have considered that maybe she needed him to write back to her, to be a strong shoulder for her to cry on. God, what a terrible time that must have been for a girl like Maddie, who'd always been the center of her parents' lives.

Carl sighed. ''There was a big scandal and a messy divorce. I don't think Maddie spoke to her daddy for quite a few years after the divorce. And of course, Nadine was a basket case, so Maddie wound up taking care of her instead of the other way around.''

''So, what's she doing now?'' Dylan asked. ''Running all of Jock's business interests, or is she leaving that up to her husband?''

Carl shook his head. ''Maddie's never married. She's been engaged twice. To that Newman boy first.

But it didn't work out. And then to some English count or duke or something. He turned out to be a penniless phony. Don't guess it's worked out too well for her. A woman with that much money could never be sure if a man was marrying her or her bank account.''

If Maddie the woman was half as fabulous as Maddie the girl, Dylan couldn't imagine a man wanting her for anything other than herself. She'd been pretty and smart and had done a real number on Dylan's teenage hormones and his young heart.

''Then I guess Maddie's the big businesswoman, huh?'' Dylan wondered if she'd cut that mane of golden-red hair and started wearing severe, nondescript business suits.

''Actually, she has a group of financial advisors and company executives that handle things for her.'' Carl finished off his fourth cup of coffee. ''Of course, she makes all final decisions, but she doesn't deal with the day-to-day running of Delarue, Inc. No, Maddie's got herself an ordinary job as the events manager over at the Lone Star Country Club, and from what I hear she's good at it, too. She's always got something going on. Take this weekend for example. She's put together some sort of black-tie murder-mystery gala. You know, one of those interactive things.''

''This weekend?''

''That's right.''

''Are you going?''

''I'd planned on it.''

''Would you like for me to go with you?''

Carl beamed. ''I'd love for you to go with me. It'd give me a chance to show you off.''

And it would give me a chance to see Maddie Delarue again, Dylan thought.

''Then we'll go and make a night of it,'' Dylan said. ''I'll wear one of my Armani tuxedos and we'll drive to the club in my Porsche. I'm having it driven here.''

Carl grinned from ear to ear. ''Can't think of anything I'd like better.''

Maddie opened the French doors that led onto the second-floor balcony. As she stepped outside, the warm summer air enveloped her and the muted hum of a midsize town at midnight drifted up from below. Her plush, ultra-modern condo was located in the center of Mission Creek, and the entire complex of luxury housing belonged to her as it once had belonged to her father. As a matter of fact, her father had kept his mistress in one of the adjacent condos, then after they married, he and Renee had lived there for almost a year before they moved out of town and resettled in Corpus Christi.

It had taken her years after the divorce to forgive her father for breaking up their family, and in time she had even learned to like her stepmother. But she'd never been able to reestablish the kind of relationship with her father that she'd wanted, mostly due to the fact that her mother expected her to choose sides.

Illumination from the town brightened the dark night like soft lights on a Christmas tree. Often she stood out here and drank in the serenity of Mission Creek in slumber, peaceful and beautiful, the cares of the day laid to rest for a few brief hours. She couldn't help thinking about all the families in all the houses in town and on the surrounding ranches. Men, women and children living perfectly normal lives and never realizing how lucky they were.

Don't do this! An inner voice commanded. Stop wallowing in self-pity.

What was wrong with her? She had a wonderful life. She was rich—filthy rich—and relatively young and quite attractive. She had a job she enjoyed. Being the country club's events manager might have started out as a lark, but over the years, it had become an integral part of Maddie's life. After all, a person could be a guest at only so many social functions, head up only so many charitable organizations, take only so many holidays abroad.

Besides, with far more knowledgeable people than she taking care of Delarue, Inc., people she trusted as her father had trusted them, Maddie needed a real job of some kind. Otherwise, she would have been available twenty-four hours a day for her mother's never-ending succession of crises.

Then again, as Nadine had said, if she had several

grandchildren to dote on, to spoil rotten, then maybe she'd have something else to concentrate on other than herself.

So, what are you going to do, Maddie, marry some money-hungry Don Juan just so your mother can have grandchildren? The very thought turned her stomach. What about artificial insemination? What about adoption? Neither solution required a husband.

Off in the distance an ambulance siren wailed. It struck a sad, sobering note in the stillness of the night. Illness? Death? Another life with problems far more serious than hers? She felt almost guilty for wanting more when she already had so much. Far more than most people. But was it too much to ask for a man who would love her and her alone? Out there somewhere, there had to be a guy, rich and successful in his own right, who could look beyond the huge Delarue fortune and see the woman who longed to be loved and cherished. A man who would teach her to trust again, to believe in the happily ever after that had eluded her parents.

Where are you? Maddie whispered. Where's the man who will sweep me off my feet and carry me away with him? Where's a guy like Dylan Bridges when you need him?

Three

Carl Bridges had handed over his caseload to another circuit court judge three days ago, the day after Dylan arrived in Mission Creek. It was that one gesture, probably more than anything else, that showed Dylan the extent of his father's love for him. He could waste time regretting the past, but he preferred to savor the present. After all, his father wasn't getting any younger and Dylan suspected Carl had problems of some sort to deal with these days. He'd noticed his dad ate antacids as if they were candy. And every time the phone ran, Carl tensed. Was he expecting news from the doctor? Dylan had tried to broach the subject of what was bothering his father, but every time he did, Carl simply dismissed his suspicions as groundless.

For some crazy reason, this evening Dylan felt like a teenager getting ready for his first date. He'd been nervous all afternoon. Whenever he thought about seeing Maddie Delarue again, he reverted to a testosterone-driven sixteen-year-old. It had been years since his body had controlled him so completely.

Dylan inspected himself in the mirror on the back

of the bathroom door. Not bad, if I do say so myself, he thought. He'd had his housekeeper FedEx one of his Armani tuxedos, along with accessories. He looked exactly like what he was—a rich, successful businessman who knew how to dress well. Gone were any remnants of the long-haired bad boy whose attire had been faded jeans and a white T-shirt. He bore only a vague resemblance to that rebellious hellion. He'd stopped wearing an earring when he was twenty-two, and over the years the hole in his ear had closed. He'd grown a few inches taller and now reached a solid six feet, and he'd put on enough weight that his once lanky frame was now toned muscle.

He doubted anyone would recognize him tonight, not even Maddie, but for the fact that he'd be showing up with his dad. How tongues would wag. What would the good townspeople be saying behind his back? Once Carl started bragging about Dylan's success, he suspected that more than one former naysayer would be surprised. He grinned at the thought. A perverse part of him wished that Jock Delarue was alive. Would Jock still think Dylan wasn't good enough for Maddie?

"Son, you certainly look handsome." Standing in the hall, just outside the bathroom, Carl surveyed Dylan. "I wish your mother were here. She'd be so proud of you."

Carl still wore his everyday clothes, a pair of khaki slacks and a short-sleeved cotton shirt.

"Dad, you aren't dressed," Dylan said. "You'd better get a move on or we'll be more than fashionably late."

"I...uh...I'm not feeling very well tonight," Carl said. "Nothing serious. I think I've picked up a bug of some sort."

"Have you called your doctor?" Dylan asked.

"No. There's no need for that. I just need to stay close to home, get a little rest. I should be fine by tomorrow."

Dylan whipped off his bow tie. "I'll change out of this tux and we'll—"

"Don't change clothes," Carl said. "I want you to go to the country club and enjoy yourself. Tell everybody there tonight who you are. And explain that you and I have reconciled our differences and the reason I didn't show up tonight is because I'm just a bit under the weather. I don't want you to miss out on the fun." Carl offered Dylan a feeble smile. "Besides, if you stay here, you won't get to see Maddie."

"What makes you think I want to see Maddie?" Dylan grinned.

"Just a calculated guess. It seems her name has come up in our conversations more than once these past few days."

Dylan shrugged. "Okay, so I'm curious about her. After all, Maddie was my first love." He laughed, but a bitter inner voice reminded him that Maddie had been his only love. The only girl who'd ever gotten under his skin.

Maddie buzzed around inside the Lone Star Country Club, issuing orders, greeting guests and double-checking everything, down to the most insignificant detail. Her detail-oriented personality lent itself well to planning and executing grand affairs. Dinner had been planned for the Empire Room, for those who came early. The Mystery Gala would be held in the ballroom on the third floor, and Maddie had assigned her new assistant, Alicia, to be in charge of the event itself, leaving Maddie free to greet guests and make sure every aspect of tonight's extravaganza went off without a hitch. An elaborate buffet table had been set up to accommodate those who hadn't dined in the Empire Room and for those wanting to snack throughout the evening.

Dressed in her simple yet elegant black gown, diamonds dripping from her ears and wrists, Maddie stood several feet from the entrance to the grand two-story, pink granite foyer. Using the tiled, granite fountain in the middle of the lobby as her backdrop, she smiled and spoke to each new arrival. From her vantage point in the lobby, she could see the cars lined up outside the club. Jaguars, Porsches, BMWs. Tonight, the elite of Mission Creek would take part in a fun and games party, and the proceeds from the event would be given to the Red Cross. Maddie especially enjoyed putting together charity events like this one, knowing that her efforts not only entertained the club's members and their friends, but also provided assistance to those in need.

Joan O'Brien, the manager of Body Perfect, the ladies' spa at the club, entered the lobby on her husband Hart's arm. Such an attractive couple, Maddie thought, and so lucky to have found each other again. Their love story was one right out of the pages of a fairy tale—or a romance novel. During the past half dozen years or so, Joan had become one of Maddie's best friends and she adored the O'Briens' nine-year-old daughter. Although she wasn't officially Helena's godmother, she adored playing the role of "Aunt" Maddie to the hilt.

No sooner had she and Joan started chatting when Hart whisked his wife away before the onslaught of the Carson clan. The big daddy of the family, Ford Carson, a robust, belly-over-his-belt type of man with a shock of white hair and bushy eyebrows, led his plump, blond wife Grace into the lobby. Following the patriarch came Flynt and Josie, Matt and Rose, then Fiona and Cara.

Seven o'clock passed quickly, turning into seven-fifteen and finally seven-thirty. Preparing to leave her post in the lobby to go upstairs to the ballroom, Maddie noticed a sleek, black Porsche pull up under the canopied entrance to the club. She wasn't sure exactly what it was about the man who stepped out of the car that attracted her attention. From this distance she couldn't make out his features clearly, but there was something about the way he carried himself, a self-confidence in his stance and walk that proclaimed to one and all that he was a man to be reckoned with. Maddie shook her head. Where had those thoughts come from? She wasn't prone to fanciful musings about perfect strangers.

Without taking another look at the intriguing man, Maddie hurried to her destination. Although the gala event didn't start until eight, the ballroom and the open-air aisles that surrounded the main area were filled with guests and busy employees. The ballroom ceiling rose two floors, and a large balcony lay directly over the two-story entrance portico. The jazz band played cool, melancholy tunes.

Maddie checked with Alicia, who assured her that she was ready, and with Harvey Small, the annoying club manager, who seemed to have his areas of expertise under control. Just as she began mingling, ever watchful for any sign of a problem, she caught a glimpse of three waitresses she now knew by name—the soft-spoken, friendly Daisy Parker, the tough-as-nails and highly efficient Ginger Walton and the irritatingly syrupy-sweet Erica Clawson. All three young ladies were attired in the white shirts and black slacks that were de rigueur for the waitstaff at the club.

While she was inspecting the buffet table, Maddie heard a discernable rumble, a soft murmuring at first that quickly turned to a loud hum. What was happening? she wondered, and turned around just in time to see the attractive man from the black Porsche standing at the entrance to the ballroom. It seemed the debonair stranger in his tailor-made tux and emitting an aura of power and success had gained the attention of almost everyone in the ballroom. Maddie's stomach flip-flopped; her nerves zinged. The guy was drop-dead gorgeous. Broad-shouldered, narrow-hipped, with short-cropped, dark blond hair and a rugged, movie-star handsome face.

Who is he? Maddie asked herself and realized that everyone here tonight was wondering the same thing. Well, whoever he was, his presence seemed to be disrupting the gala before it even began. Doing her duty, she sailed across the room and made her way directly to the man who was now watching her approach. His hot gaze raked over her, searing her with its intensity. She suddenly felt as if he'd stripped her naked. Since vulnerability was not a word Maddie allowed in her vocabulary, she returned his gaze head-on. As she drew nearer, she realized he was grinning—at her. Was he someone she should know?

"Hello, I'm Maddie Delarue. Welcome to the Lone Star Country Club." Her heart beat an erratic rat-a-tat-tat as she extended her hand. "I'm the club's events manager and your hostess for tonight's party."

The moment he touched her, a tingle of electricity zipped up her arm and radiated throughout her body.

Oh, dear, this wouldn't do. She'd never had this type of reaction to a man.

"Well, hello, Maddie Delarue," he said, his voice deep and husky, a definite baritone.

Maddie realized that people were still buzzing with speculation and many were staring directly at them. Defuse this situation, she told herself. She boosted her courage with determination and laced her arm though the stranger's. "This is a private party, Mr.…er…" When he didn't supply a name, she continued. "By invitation only. I assume you aren't a party-crasher."

"Oh, no," he replied. "I'm a lot of things, beautiful Maddie, but a party-crasher is not one of them."

She tingled from head to toe. Get a grip, girl, she warned herself. It's not as if this is the first man who's ever tried to sweet-talk you. You've heard insincere compliments before, numerous times. But oddly enough she believed this man really did think she was beautiful.

As she led him into the ballroom, she asked, "Since you're not a party-crasher, would you care to enumerate some of the things you are?"

Towering over her five-foot-four height, he stopped suddenly and clasped her hand. Taken aback by his bold action when he brought her hand to his mouth and kissed her tenderly just above her knuckles, she glowered at him. This guy was suave, sophisticated and doing his level best to impress her. She knew his type only too well, and yet this man seemed different from the regular run-of-the-mill Don Juan.

"Let me see, sweet Maddie." He smiled; she glared. "I'm a connoisseur of fine wine, of artwork that appeals to me, of the ballet and the opera and of—" he paused for effect "—beautiful women."

"My, how interesting. I've known quite a few men who are just that type of connoisseur." He cocked his eyebrows; she smiled. "That type is usually also a hunter—" she paused for effect "—a fortune hunter."

The stranger laughed. A hearty, deep-chested rumble. "I can assure you, Ms. Delarue, that I have no interest in or need of your sizable fortune."

"Is that right?" Suddenly she realized that their lengthy conversation was attracting more attention than the stranger's entrance had. She followed her first instinct—to take him away from prying eyes. "Why don't I show you the view from the balcony? You can see for miles. It's quite a spectacular sight."

"Lead the way."

He draped her arm over his and obediently followed her halfway across the room, then abruptly took a detour and all but dragged her onto the dance floor. Had it not been for creating a scene, she would have responded rather sternly to the man's brazen tactics. Forcing herself not to stomp on his feet, she allowed him to take her into his arms and guide her through the slow, seductive dance steps. His hand drifted down her back to her waist. She sucked in her breath, then released it slowly when he nuzzled the side of her face with his nose.

"Just exactly who are you and what are you doing here tonight?" She managed to speak without her voice quivering, which amazed her since her insides had turned to mush. Her nipples tightened and peaked. Her femininity moistened. This guy was lethal!

"Ah, straight to the point," he said. "Have you decided that there's no longer any need to be polite?"

"I'm politely asking you a few questions," she told him.

His hand strayed lower, coming to a halt at the base of her spine. She lifted her hand from his shoulder, reached behind her and grabbed his wrist. When she tried to move his splayed hand upward, he resisted and instead dragged his hand and hers down and onto one satin-clad buttock. Maddie gasped.

"Let go of me," she ordered. "Don't touch me that way. People are watching us."

Chuckling, he raised his hand back to her waist; she returned hers to his shoulder. "Better?" he asked.

"Yes, thank you, much better."

"As for who I am and what I'm doing here...I'm an invited guest who came here to enjoy himself, and I'm certainly doing just that dancing with you."

Maddie rolled her eyes. "We aim to please."

"Do you indeed?"

"Only in my capacity as your hostess," she amended her statement.

"Of course."

Don't you dare blush, Maddie warned herself. If he saw evidence that his flirting was affecting her, he'd assume she was vulnerable to his charm. She'd dance this one dance with him. That was all. Then she'd dismiss him from her thoughts. But as the dance continued, her body betrayed her by molding itself to his, fitting them together like two halves of a whole.

"Do you really have an invitation?" she asked.

"Yes."

"May I see it?"

"I left it with the gentleman at the door."

"Oh."

The music ended and before the band began the next melody, he took her hand and led her off the dance floor and straight toward the doors that opened up onto the balcony. Her mind warned her to resist, to put a stop to his take-charge maneuver. But her instincts, primed by an odd sense of anticipation and curiosity, kept her at his side. Once on the balcony, where only a handful of guests mingled in quiet, dark corners, Maddie pulled free of the stranger and asked, "What sort of game are you playing?"

He grinned. "Do you like games? You must, to spend your life planning things that entertain a bunch of rich, bored Texans."

"The Mystery Gala happens to be a charity event, with proceeds going to the Red Cross. If you received an invitation, then you know that you were expected to make a sizable donation for the privilege of participating in tonight's event.''

''I'm here as a guest of a Lone Star Country Club member,'' he told her.

''And just who might that be?''

Before she realized what was happening, he pulled her into his arms. ''Still the same cautious yet curious Maddie.''

''What?'' She looked up, because even wearing three-inch heels, she wasn't at eye-level with him.

''You honestly don't remember me, do you?''

''Am I supposed to know you?''

He lowered his head. She held her breath. His lips brushed hers softly, tentatively. She sighed. You're insane if you let him kiss you, she told herself. But when his mouth covered hers, she disregarded the warning and participated fully in the experience. His kiss possessed an equal combination of passion and tenderness that ignited a longing within her like none she'd ever known. Strangely enough, the only other kiss that had ever come close to matching this one was the time Dylan Bridges had— Dylan Bridges! My God! Could it be?

Breathless and stunned by the possibility, she jerked away from the stranger and surveyed him from head to toe.

''Honey, you reacted to that kiss the same way you reacted to the one I gave you seventeen years ago.''

His smile widened, revealing a set of straight white teeth.

Dylan Bridges! Had she known, subconsciously, who he was? Physically he bore only a slight resemblance to the sixteen-year-old boy she remembered. Gone was the long, pale blond hair, the gold earring, the grungy jeans and tattered T-shirt. He was taller, broader, and an air of alluring self-confidence had replaced the cocky bravado he'd once displayed.

Not giving a thought to her actions, guided by pure feminine instinct, Maddie grabbed the lapels of Dylan's tuxedo and kissed him. She had to find out if another kiss would affect her the same way the first kiss had seventeen years ago, the way the one tonight had. Pure dynamite. Explosions erupted throughout her body and inside her head as she threw her arms around his neck and deepened the kiss. He took his lead from her and within minutes he backed her up against the brick wall, positioned his erection against her flat belly and devoured her mouth with his. The hunger inside her raged, needing to be fed.

The sound of voices brought Maddie out of the sensual haze that had momentarily overcome her common sense. Taking several deep, calming breaths, she pulled away from him.

"I—I don't know what made me do that," she said.

"Don't you?"

She blushed. Dammit, she hadn't blushed in ages. "Sexual chemistry, I guess," Maddie admitted.

"Yeah, we seem to still have plenty of that, don't we?"

She blew out a long, I-need-to-take-control-of-my-emotions breath. "What are you doing here?"

"In Mission Creek or at the country club tonight?"

"Both."

"I came home to visit my father," Dylan told her. "Dad and I decided it was time to put the past behind us and see if we can build a new and better father/son relationship."

"That's wonderful. I'm sure your father is very pleased," she said. "Where is Carl tonight? I know he was on our guest list."

"Dad wasn't feeling well. He thinks he might have caught a bug, but he insisted I come to the Mystery Gala without him." Dylan looked deeply into her eyes. "He knew how much I wanted to see you again."

Dylan's statement figuratively and literally took her breath away. "Oh," was all she could manage to say.

"You're even prettier than I remembered," he said. "Maturity becomes you, Maddie."

"It does you, too. I didn't even recognize you. You look so different."

"Thanks. I did some growing up at the Reform Center for Boys and a lot more growing up after I got out and tried to make it on my own."

She glanced at his expensive tuxedo. "Apparently, you've done all right."

"Well enough. What about you? What's the richest woman in Texas doing working as the events manager for the Lone Star Country Club? Whatever happened to Daddy's spoiled darling?"

"The spoiled little princess you knew doesn't exist anymore. The woman I am today likes her job here at the club. And if I do say so myself, I'm damn good at it." She glanced into the ballroom. "And speaking of my job—I need to go back inside and see to it that this evening's party goes as planned."

"You don't have a date tonight, do you?"

"No, I don't, but—"

"You do now."

Dylan took her arm, escorted her into the ballroom and didn't leave her side for the next hour while she kept watch over the proceedings. Before the staged murder occurred and the mystery solving began, Maddie introduced Dylan to all the Carsons in attendance, as well as several Wainwrights and a couple he didn't know—Joan and Hart O'Brien. Dylan had repeated the same explanation numerous times. Carl was home with a virus of some sort. He and his father were in the process of patching up their relationship. Yes, he'd be in town for a while. He lived and worked in Dallas. He was a stockbroker, and yes, he'd turned his life around after his two years in the Texas Reform Center for Boys.

Dylan pulled Maddie aside. "Looks like your assistant can handle things here. How about you and I slip away for a while?''

''Allowing Alicia to take charge of tonight's gala is part of my training strategy. I believe hands-on experience is the best way to learn. But even though she's doing a wonderful job, I'm not sure I'd feel comfortable leaving her completely on her own.''

Dylan tugged on Maddie's arm. ''Let's go. We won't be gone long. Half an hour.''

''I don't think so.''

''Come on, Maddie. You know you're dying to come with me.''

Before she had a chance to reply, he whisked her out of the ballroom, down to the lobby and outside to the covered portico. He asked the valet for his car and while they waited, he watched Maddie.

''Stop looking at me like that,'' she told him.

''Like what?''

''Like I'm the first woman you've seen in ten years.''

''I haven't seen you in seventeen years.''

A warm flush spread through Maddie's body. Why was it that Dylan had a way of saying things that affected her in a sexual way? His words went to her head the way champagne did, producing a similar intoxication.

''Thirty minutes. That's all,'' she told him. ''I shouldn't be leaving the party this way, but—''

"But you couldn't resist me any more tonight than you were able to when we were sixteen."

The valet brought the black Porsche to a halt in front of the country club. Maddie eyed the car suspiciously.

"Yours?" she asked.

"Mine," he replied.

"Not borrowed?"

He chuckled. "Bought and paid for. The bill of sale is in the glove compartment, if you'd like to check."

Dylan tipped the valet generously, then shooed him aside when he opened the passenger door for Maddie. Dylan assisted her into the car, then rounded the hood and hopped in behind the wheel. He revved the motor, flew down the circular drive and out onto the open road.

The evening breeze assaulted Maddie's hair, which tonight she'd worn in a sophisticated French twist. Tendrils eased free; some curled about her face and others stuck to her cheeks. She'd look windblown and mussed by the time they returned to the club, but she didn't care. Lately she'd been daydreaming of a man like Dylan Bridges coming into her life and sweeping her off her feet. Little had she realized that the man himself would re-enter her life and make her experience daring, dizzying feelings that prompted her to throw caution to the wind. A thirty-minute escape wouldn't hurt her. She could allow herself that much time away from reality, couldn't she?

Maddie reached up, removed the pins from her hair, shook her head and let her long tresses fall free. In her peripheral vision she caught a glimpse of Dylan stealing a quick glance at her. She tossed back her head and laughed. Leaving behind responsibilities and uncertainties, she raced off into the dark Texas night with a man she'd known only as a teenage rebel.

Dear God, when was the last time she'd felt this good, and so totally alive with anticipation?

Four

Dylan had a difficult time keeping his eyes on the road. Of all the women he'd known in his thirty-three years, Maddie Delarue was one of a kind. She was not only the most beautiful, but the most tempting. Yeah, sure, part of the fascination was the fact she'd been the star of his adolescent wet dreams, the girl he'd fantasized about scoring with, the forbidden fruit he hadn't been able to resist trying to pick. But what the hell did he really know about the woman she was now? Not a damn thing other than she had enough money to buy and sell anybody in Mission Creek, including the Wainwrights and Carsons. And he knew one other thing—he still had the hots for her. How was that possible?

He'd recognized her instantly, the moment he'd seen her standing in the country club lobby, looking like some fairy-tale princess in her chic black gown and her sparkling diamonds. By the time she'd rushed over to him when he entered the ballroom, he was fighting to tame his body's reaction. He hadn't gotten that aroused that fast since he'd been twenty.

"Where are we going?" Maddie asked.

"Does it matter?"

"No, I suppose it doesn't. Just remember you promised to get me back to the club in thirty minutes."

"Then we can't go far," he said. "I seem to remember a bumpy dirt road not far from here. Is it still there?"

Maddie laughed. "You've got to be kidding. Do you really want to take a ride down Memory Lane?"

"Yeah, why not? I'd kind of like to see how things would've turned out seventeen years ago if the police hadn't shown up."

"I'm not sure," she told him, "but I think I might have gone all the way with you. You were pretty heady stuff for an innocent like me. Your kisses really curled my toes. I'd never experienced anything so powerful."

"Lady, you know how to turn the screws, don't you?" He grinned at her, even though he was hurting in the worst possible way. "You've got to know that telling a guy something like that is bound to increase the size of his ego...and certain vital parts of his body."

"Are you referring to a swollen head?" she taunted.

"Red, you're shameless. You know damn well it's not my head that's swollen."

Maddie burst into laughter. Dylan loved the sound. It was refreshingly genuine. Just like the woman herself. He'd dated so many phonies, so many women who pretended to be something they weren't, that being with a woman as open and honest as Maddie aroused him unbearably. He felt he could see right through her, as if she had no defenses, as if she'd lowered her protective shield and allowed him a glimpse at the real woman beneath the polished exterior.

"There's an overlook on the ridge," Maddie said, a wide smile on her face. "It won't take ten minutes to get there and the view is magnificent. Just take Goldenrod Road for about two miles. I'll tell you where to turn."

"Is this a lover's lane?" he asked.

"I don't think so. It's on private property and is posted with signs stating that fact."

"Are you trying to get me in trouble with the law again?" he asked teasingly.

"The land belongs to me," she replied.

"Ah, I should have known. Just another part of Delarue, Inc.'s vast holdings."

"A very small part."

He turned off onto Goldenrod Road and checked the mileage gauge. "So, why did you decide not to take over the reins of Delarue, Inc., when your father died?"

"Oh, but I did take over. At least for a while. I found out rather quickly that I hadn't inherited any ruthless, cutthroat genes from my father, personality traits necessary to command a business empire the size of Delarue, Inc.'' Maddie looked straight ahead, taking note of the passing scenery, visible by the light of the three-quarter moon. ''I have a say in whatever major decisions are made, but I prefer to leave the day-to-day running of the business to men and women who thrive on it.''

''I'm surprised you didn't find yourself a husband who would've loved to take charge.''

''Turn left at the next four-way stop,'' she told him. ''Are you applying for the position?''

Dylan stopped at the four-way intersection, and not seeing another vehicle in any direction, he idled the Porsche and turned his gaze on Maddie. ''Is that what you think this is all about? You think I'm interested in getting my hands on Delarue, Inc.?''

''You tell me.'' Maddie stared directly into his eyes. ''I heard you telling people that you're a stockbroker in Dallas, which tells me that you're a shrewd businessman. Shrewd enough to afford a Porsche and an Armani suit and a Rolex watch and—''

He reached across the console, lifted his hand to her face and caressed her cheek. ''I don't need Delarue, Inc. I don't want Delarue, Inc. I've got more money than I'll spend in two lifetimes.''

''Then you're very rich?''

''Not as rich as you, but then few people are.'' He ran the tip of his index finger across her slightly parted lips. ''I'm a multimillionaire and I get richer every day. I seem to have the Midas touch when it comes to making money."

Dylan returned his hands to the steering wheel, switched on the blinker to indicate a left turn, then headed the Porsche down the dark country road. Neither he nor Maddie said a word as they drove along the winding lane that led to the ridge overlooking the valley. He pulled his car up to the edge of the paved overlook and parked, but left the motor running. He punched the CD player and instantly the still night air filled with hauntingly sweet jazz.

"So, if you're not interested in my money, what are you interested in?" Maddie asked, keeping her gaze focused straight ahead at the starry summer night sky.

"Honey, do you really need to ask me that?"

"Yes, I'm afraid I do."

"Been bushwhacked a few times, have you? One gigolo too many?"

"Something like that. You remember Jimmy Don Newman, don't you? Well, I was engaged to him briefly when I was nineteen. All of two weeks. I found him in bed with my college roommate and he laughed in my face. He told me that the only reason he'd ever dated me was because I was the heiress to the Delarue fortune."

"Son of a bitch."

"Yes, he was. And my only regret is that I wasted so much of my time with him. But Jimmy Don wasn't half the cad my second fiancé was. Nigel Pennington, the Earl of Cimberleigh, latched on to me when I vacationed in Europe the summer after I received my master's degree. It was my first vacation without my mother and I must admit that I was raring to do something wild and fun. Nigel wasn't very wild, but he was a lot of fun."

"So what happened with dear old Nigel?"

"On the night of our engagement party, which took place at the castle of some friend of his, I inadvertently discovered that not only was Nigel knee-deep in debt, he already had a fiancée. The woman was posing as his devoted sister."

"You're right. I believe Nigel's duplicity tops Jimmy Don's."

"There have been a few others," she admitted. "Not fiancés, just temporary boyfriends. And not a one of them could see anything except dollar signs when they looked at me."

"Then they were fools."

"Dylan, don't. I'm not good at playing games, so I gave up playing them quite a few years ago."

"The only game I want to play with you is good old-fashioned Post Office. It's a game where I kiss you and you kiss me back."

"Aren't we a little old to be playing a kid's game?"

"The way I play it, it's a very grown-up game." Dylan reached over, swooped her out of her seat, across the console and into his lap.

Déjà vu.

''I seem to remember your doing this once before,'' she said, sitting stiffly atop his thighs.

He kissed her neck. ''Do you remember my doing this?''

''No.''

He skimmed his fingertips over the rise of her breasts exposed by the low, square-cut neckline of her satin gown. ''What about this?''

''No.''

He forked his splayed fingers through her wind-tousled hair and held her head in place as he lowered his mouth to hers. With his lips a hairbreadth from hers, he said, ''But you remember this, don't you?''

''Yes.''

The kiss was as hard and demanding as the one the sixteen-year-old Dylan had given her, but with the expertise of a man who had perfected the art of kissing with years of experience. He could tell that she was thinking about resisting him, but suddenly, as if something bold and daring broke free inside her, she gave herself over completely to the moment. When she softened against him, he absorbed her, melding her flesh to his. He teased and tasted, delved and retreated. And all the while he held her head in place, a part of him was afraid she might pull away. Lost in the throes of fulfilling a teenage boy's fantasy, Dylan didn't realize that he was fast losing control, as if his sixteen-year-old self had taken possession of his thirty-three-year-old mind and body. When he cupped one of her breasts through the satin material of her gown, Maddie whimpered, which drove him crazy.

While he ravaged her mouth, he slid his hand over her back, seeking the gown's zipper. When he eased the zipper open, Maddie moved against his chest and mumbled against his lips.

"Stop, Dylan. Please, stop."

Damn! He jerked up the zipper, stopped kissing her and buried his face against her bare shoulder. After taking several deep breaths, he lifted his head and looked directly at her.

"I'm sorry, Maddie. I didn't mean to let things get out of hand." He grinned sheepishly. "I don't usually lose control like that."

Maddie eased up and out of his lap, slid across the console and back into the passenger seat. Breathing raggedly, she hugged her arms across her waist.

"You didn't do anything I didn't want you to do," she admitted. "The truth is I'd really like to...have sex with you. But I'm not going to. I've sworn off men. And, Dylan Bridges, you're most definitely a man. As much as I'd like to believe that you're my fantasy come true, you aren't. And despite the fact that we knew each other in high school, you're really a stranger to me now."

Dylan ran his hand over his face and down his throat, then looked up at the starry night sky. "I'm going to be in Mission Creek for a while. I'd like to see you again."

"We'd better not start something that is bound to end badly for both of us," she told him. "Besides, you should be spending all your time with your father."

"I don't think Dad would mind if I had a few dates while I'm here. Besides, I've been seriously considering moving back to Mission Creek for good."

Maddie jerked her head around and stared at him. "You have? But why would you want to leave Dallas?"

"Because my dad's here." He could have added "because you're here," but he didn't. Maddie Delarue would find out soon enough that she hadn't seen the last of him.

"Yes, of course. I understand. You two have spent years apart."

She looked at Dylan, her blue eyes filled with sympathy. The last thing—the very last thing—he wanted from this woman was sympathy. He wanted to be her friend and her lover, not necessarily in that order. But he didn't want to be a guy she felt sorry for, as she had when they'd been kids.

Dylan checked his Rolex. "I think our thirty minutes are up."

"Yes, I'm sure they are."

He shifted the car into reverse and headed down the ridge. Maddie remained quiet and Dylan couldn't think of anything else to say. At least not tonight. But she'd be hearing from him again—sooner rather than later. Tomorrow he'd start with a dozen roses. Not red ones. Not for Maddie. Peach roses. To match her peaches-and-cream skin and her peachy golden-red hair.

Within ten minutes, he drove under the canopied entrance portico at the country club. After getting out and tossing his keys to the valet, he rounded the hood and opened Maddie's door. As they walked into the lobby, Maddie paused.

"I need to freshen up before I return to the ballroom. Why don't you go on back to the party? I'll see you later."

Dylan grasped her hand. "Let me take you to dinner tomorrow night." Dammit, man, you're rushing her, he told himself. You should have waited. What's the matter with you? Can't you control your impulses where Maddie is concerned?

She shook her head. "Ask anyone who knows me and they'll tell you that Maddie Delarue doesn't do relationships. I'm lousy at them. I don't believe in love and happily ever after."

"I'm not asking for a relationship. Just a date, to start with. And then later on, when you're ready—"

"Sex?"

He grinned. "Yeah, Red, sex would be nice."

"Just sex?"

"Sure. Just sex."

Her fragile smile bothered him greatly. Once again he could see beyond the facade she presented so bravely and saw the lonely woman beneath. Poor little rich girl, he thought, and he had the oddest notion that he was the one man on earth who could make Maddie happy.

He wanted her more than he'd ever wanted anything. And by God, he meant to have her. In the past ten years he'd gotten just about everything he'd wanted. Perhaps that rate of success had spoiled him, made him believe he was invincible when he wasn't. But Maddie was worth the effort, worth the risk of falling flat on his face.

"Please, leave me alone," Maddie said. "I'm used to my life the way it is. I'm not willing to jeopardize my security and peace of mind for an ill-fated romance. I don't have room in my life for a reformed bad boy, no matter how tempting he is."

Dylan released her hand. "Who says I'm reformed?" He turned and walked away, leaving her in the lobby as he went upstairs to rejoin the party.

Maddie entered the ballroom ten minutes later. She had brushed her hair, having no choice but to leave it hanging loose, and she'd reapplied her makeup, hoping no one would notice that her lips were slightly swollen. As she walked into the room, she glanced around, looking for Dylan. If he was here, she didn't see him. The local actor playing the part of the police detective had rounded up what he was referring to as the "usual suspects" in the fictitious murder case.

Maddie maneuvered around the edges of the room until she made her way to Alicia.

"How's it going?" Maddie asked.

"Beautifully. Everyone is having such a good time, including me." Alicia glanced at Maddie and smiled, then did a double take as she stared at Maddie's hair.

"The French twist was so tight it gave me a headache," Maddie said in way of explanation. "So, do you think you're ready for the next big event here at the club? We really should start planning the Labor Day barbeque as soon as possible."

"Yes, we should. And I have a few ideas I'd like to go over with— Drat, there's Mr. Small motioning to me. He's been the one unpleasant aspect of this entire evening. He keeps giving me suggestions, as if he's my boss instead of you."

Maddie laughed as she glanced at the short, squat man who tried to rule the club with an iron fist. Poor Harvey. If a person could buy Harvey for what he was worth, then sell him for what he thought he was worth, that person could make a fortune. "Better you deal with him than me. Go on over there and see what he wants. And humor the man, at least until this party ends."

"Yes, ma'am, I'll do my best."

Using a microphone to broadcast this part of the ongoing fictitious murder mystery, the actor playing Detective Madison interrogated Flynt Carson, while Archy Wainwright's godson, Joe Turner, stood at his side, waiting his turn to be questioned about the make-believe murder of a man named Jeffrey Hughes.

''Just where were you when Mr. Hughes was shot?'' Detective Madison inquired. ''And just how well did you know Mrs. Hughes? I've been told that you and she are secret lovers.''

Flynt couldn't keep a straight face, but he tried not to laugh as he replied, ''Somebody's been filling your head with a pack of lies, Detective. I'm a one-woman man.'' Flynt glanced across the room at a smiling Josie, who sat with his parents, and seemed to be enjoying the good-natured fun as much as her husband.

Suddenly Detective Madison turned to Joe. ''And what about you, Mr. Turner? Where were you at approximately five after nine tonight? And isn't it true that Mr. Hughes cheated you out of a great deal of money on a land development deal recently?''

''I have an alibi,'' Joe said, a hint of a grin playing at the corners of his mouth. ''I was with Flynt and he was with me, so you'd better find yourself somebody else to question.''

Everyone burst into gales of laughter. Detective Madison scratched his bald head, then playing right along with the game, returned his accusatory gaze to Flynt. ''You're a rich man, Mr. Carson. Just how much did you pay Joe Turner to lie and give you an alibi?''

While the game continued, Maddie made an inspection of the buffet table and reminded the jazz band what music to play when the ''killer'' was identified, then she rescued Alicia from Harvey. And as she went about her duties, she searched for Dylan. Where was he? She'd thought he planned to return to the ballroom when she'd left him to go to the ladies' room nearly fifteen minutes ago. Had he changed his mind and gone home?

''There's that handsome man everyone's been talking about,'' Alicia said.

Maddie's heartbeat accelerated. ''Where?''

''There.'' Alicia nodded toward the entrance to the ballroom. ''I think he's looking for someone.''

Maddie tried not to glance his way, but need overruled subtlety. With a good twenty feet separating them, their gazes met and locked. Maddie's breath caught in her throat. How in the world was she going to resist Dylan, when what she wanted more than anything was to run to him and throw herself into his arms?

Idiot, she chided herself. You're asking for trouble if you buy into the fantasy that Dylan is the one man on earth who will love you for yourself. You've been fooled before and gotten your heart broken. But if you're stupid enough to let him manipulate you, you deserve whatever you get.

If Dylan broke her heart, Maddie knew she might not ever recover.

''Watch out, there goes Fiona Carson into action,''

Alicia said. "I wondered how long it would take her to zero in on Mr. Fabulous."

Maddie watched while the lovely Fiona sashayed up to Dylan and began flirting with him. Dylan broke eye contact with Maddie, then turned his considerable charm on the wild and luscious Carson twin who went through men as if they were disposable tissues. An unwanted, sickening feeling of jealousy came to life inside Maddie. She knew such feelings were ridiculous; after all, Dylan Bridges didn't mean anything to her. She had no claims on him. He was certainly free to romance any woman he wanted.

As the evening wore on, Maddie deliberately avoided Dylan, who had attracted several other single ladies. However, when any of those other women ventured forward, Fiona quite efficiently dismissed them. From time to time, Maddie caught Dylan staring at her and whenever he noticed her looking at him, he'd grin and wink. Devil! Maybe he wasn't such a reformed character after all. Apparently there was still quite a bit of bad boy left in him. And that was probably what had attracted Fiona. Well, let Fiona have him. Fiona Carson wasn't the type who'd let any man break her heart.

With the murder mystery solved and a sputtering middle-aged actor carted off to jail, overacting his part as the killer, the crowd began milling around, a few preparing to leave, while others hit the dance floor or entered the buffet line. Maddie watched while the waitresses refilled the silver chafing dishes that lined the elegant table.

Joan O'Brien came up beside Maddie and handed her a flute of champagne. "Where did you disappear to earlier this evening?"

"I stepped out for a breath of fresh air."

"With Dylan Bridges?"

Maddie gasped, then laughed. "We had some old business to take care of."

"I see." Joan inclined her head toward Dylan and Fiona on the dance floor. "So, what's Fiona—new business?"

"I wouldn't know. And I don't care."

"You wouldn't lie to your best friend, would you?"

"I'm not—"

The shrill screams rent the still night air. From somewhere outside, a woman's bloodcurdling shrieks stopped everyone dead in their tracks.

"What on earth...?" Joan stared at Maddie.

The band continued playing, but the dancers stopped and joined the others as they questioned the location of the screams and the identity of the woman. Maddie headed for the raised dais on which the band presided. She had to take charge of this situation before anyone panicked.

Gripping the microphone tightly in her hand, she said, "Ladies and gentlemen, please stay calm. I'm sure very shortly we'll have an explanation about what's going on. I'm on my way downstairs to find out what has happened.''

If the actors she'd hired for tonight's performance had taken it upon themselves to improvise something extra for her guests' entertainment, she'd let them know she didn't appreciate their upsetting everyone this way.

Before Maddie made it across the ballroom and to the door, Harvey Small and the actor who had played Detective Madison rushed into the room. Harvey's round, fat face was pale, and his beady brown eyes bugged out with sheer horror.

''There's been a murder,'' Harvey said. ''A real murder. There's a body floating in the pond in front of the club.''

Murmurs mixed with shocked cries. Maddie drew in a deep breath.

''Who was that screaming?'' someone asked.

''Who got killed?'' another inquired.

''Erica Clawson, one of our waitresses, had gone outside for a smoke,'' Harvey said, his voice trembling slightly. ''She—she discovered the body.''

''Whose body?'' Ford Carson asked as he made his way forward through the throng of party-goers.

Harvey swallowed hard, then looked right at Dylan, who stood, with Fiona on his arm, only a few feet away from her parents. ''It's Judge Bridges. Judge Carl Bridges.''

Five

At first Maddie couldn't move, couldn't think, could barely breathe. Carl Bridges was dead? Murdered? No, it wasn't possible. Harvey had to be wrong. It couldn't be Carl. Not now when Dylan had just returned to Mission Creek to rebuild a relationship with his father.

Dylan! Oh, God, Dylan!

Turning quickly, Maddie moved toward Dylan, who stood stiffly, a dazed expression on his face. Was he in shock? she wondered. Then abruptly, as if he'd suddenly understood what Harvey had said, as if reality had broken through the veil of disbelief, Dylan ran out of the ballroom.

"Have you called the police?" Justin Wainwright, the local sheriff who'd been attending tonight's gala, questioned Harvey.

"I did that immediately," Harvey replied, then motioned toward the door by which Dylan had just left. "Wasn't that Carl Bridges' prodigal son running out of here? Sheriff, you might want to catch him before he gets away."

"I'm sure Dylan isn't running away," Maddie said.

''He probably wants to see for himself that his father is dead.''

''With their past history I'd say that Dylan Bridges should be a prime suspect.'' Harvey puffed out his rotund chest. ''The whole town knows that father and son haven't spoken to each other in years.''

Maddie glowered at the roly-poly manager. ''Why don't you shut up, Harvey? You don't know what you're talking about.''

Hart O'Brien, who was a detective on the Mission Creek police force, stepped forward. ''Let's not panic, folks. And let's not start pointing fingers. Until officers on duty show up, I guess I'll be taking charge of this situation.''

Maddie had to find Dylan, had to go to him and help him if she could. While speculations of who might have killed Carl and why surfaced in the crowd, several of the men made their way downstairs. Maddie rushed past the men, disregarding the sounds of her mother's hysterical voice and Joan calling her name. She'd deal with her mother later, and she knew Joan was simply concerned about her.

When Maddie reached the lobby, she saw two Lone Star Country Club security guards holding Dylan back, away from the pond. Emotion clogged Maddie's throat. Oh, Dylan...Dylan. Forcing her trembling legs to move, she hurried outside, across the circular drive and toward the small crowd of people who had congregated around the pond. Some were club members, others employees.

''Let me go!'' Dylan struggled with the guards. ''That's my father in there. Please, for God's sake, let me go to him.''

''I'm sorry, sir,'' one of the guards—Curt Dodd—said. ''But our orders are to keep the crime scene secure until the police arrive.''

Maddie came up behind the guards. ''Curt, please release Mr. Bridges. He's simply upset about his father. I'm sure you can understand what he's feeling right now.''

''Are you going to stay put?'' Curt asked Dylan.

Dylan nodded, and Curt released him.

Maddie eased over to Dylan's side and laid her hand on his shoulder. He snapped his head around and looked at her, his eyes glistening with unshed tears.

''It's him, Maddie,'' Dylan said. ''That's my father lying there in that pond and they won't let me go to him.''

Maddie ventured a glance, then winced when she saw Judge Bridges' body floating face-up in the pond. He wore slacks and a short-sleeved shirt that had probably been blue, but was now stained a vivid red. There was blood all over the upper part of his torso, and the water surrounding him showed evidence of where his life's blood had drained from him and tinted the pond a deadly red.

''Who'd want to kill my dad?''

Maddie thought Dylan sounded like a little boy, and hearing that vulnerability made her want to wrap her arms around him and offer him comfort. But before she could act on her instincts, Hart O'Brien walked past them and took a look at the murder scene.

"The chief's on his way over here now," Hart said. "I'm afraid no one can leave until we've questioned each person here tonight."

"You might as well start with the most likely suspect," Harvey Small shouted. "Ask Dylan Bridges to account for every minute of his time tonight. He most certainly wasn't at the party the entire evening."

"Why don't you keep quiet, Harvey?" Justin Wainwright said. "I think Hart and I can handle things without your assistance or interference."

"Well, I'm just stating the obvious." Harvey huffed. "Everybody in and around Mission Creek knows that Dylan Bridges hated his father because the judge didn't do anything to stop him from being sent to a reform center. Maybe he came back to Mission Creek for revenge."

Maddie slipped away from Dylan's side and marched over to Harvey. She spoke softly, keeping a mild expression on her face. "If you say one more word about Dylan Bridges, I will personally see to it that you're fired from the club. And I'll make sure no one in Texas will ever give you another job. Do I make myself clear, Mr. Small?"

Harvey swallowed. He narrowed his gaze and pursed his lips. "You have no right to—"

Maddie grabbed his arm. "You do not want to make an enemy of me."

Harvey tensed. Maddie released his arm. He stepped away from her and kept his mouth shut.

Hart bent over the edge of the pond and inspected the body, then reached down and touched it. Dylan took a tentative step toward the pond. When Curt Dodd made a move to grab Dylan, Hart held up his hand and signaled for the security guard to leave Dylan alone.

"I'm sorry, Mr. Bridges," Hart said. "But it looks like your father took a couple of bullets in the chest." Then Hart spoke to Justin, but his voice carried on the nighttime air. "From what I could make out, I'd say the shooting happened fairly recently. Rigor mortis hasn't set in yet and the body isn't cold."

"I hear sirens now," Justin said. "I imagine that's the chief. Why don't I get everybody back inside before he gets here? You'll have your hands full out here."

"Yeah, thanks," Hart said.

Dylan refused to go. "I want to stay," he said.

"All right," Hart replied. "But back away from the pond. Mr. Bridges, do you know of anyone who might have wanted to harm the judge?"

Dylan shook his head. "I have no idea. My father

and I have been out of touch for years...until recently.''

''Then what Harvey Small said about you is true?''

''The part about my past history with my father is true,'' Dylan admitted. ''But believe me, I didn't do this. I'd never—'' Dylan's voice cracked.

Maddie rushed to him, clutched his arm and said to Hart, ''When Dylan left the party tonight, I was with him. We went for a drive. So, you see, he has an alibi...if he needs one.''

''Mmm-hmm.'' Hart looked down at his feet. ''Were you with Mr. Bridges the entire time he was absent from the party?''

''Yes, I—'' Maddie had been willing to lie for Dylan.

''No, she wasn't,'' Dylan said. ''I was alone for about fifteen minutes.'' His gaze met Maddie's and she saw great sadness in his eyes. ''When Maddie...Ms. Delarue and I returned from our drive, I took a walk around the club and got a little fresh air before I went back to the ballroom.''

''Did anyone see you?'' Hart asked.

''As far as I know, not a soul.''

A maroon Chevy Blazer pulled to a screeching halt in the country club's circular drive. Chief of Police Burl Terry jumped out and came barreling toward the pond, two officers scurrying behind him like eager-to-please puppies. Following the massive arrests in the Mission Creek police department several months ago,

Terry, a straight-arrow, bulldog cop from Houston, had been hired to take over Ben Stone's position, after the corrupt chief had been killed.

Terry started barking orders as he marched around the pond. A police photographer snapped photo after photo.

When the ambulance arrived a few minutes later, Hart came over to Maddie. "Why don't you take Mr. Bridges inside and get him a cup of coffee?"

"All right." But when Maddie tugged on Dylan's arm, he balked.

"I want my father's killer found," Dylan said.

"Then we want the same thing," Hart replied. "Once we finish up out here, I'm sure the chief will want you to come downtown with us. Just to answer a few questions. You might know something that can help us."

Dylan shrugged. "You don't have to tell me not to leave town. I'm not going anywhere until the person who murdered my father is found and brought to justice." Dylan jerked away from Maddie. "I appreciate your trying to help me, but you don't want to get involved with a bad boy like me. Not again. Ironic, isn't it, that every time you hook up with me, you wind up being questioned by the police?"

"Dylan, I—"

"Run, honey. Run like hell before you get dragged into this mess with me."

She stared at him, not knowing what to say or do,

but when she heard her mother's voice crying out her name, she turned and walked across the driveway. The last thing Dylan needed was having to listen to Nadine Delarue's rantings. When she approached her mother, who was being restrained by Joan O'Brien, Maddie gave her friend an appreciative glance, then faced Nadine's displeasure.

"What do you mean defending that young hoodlum?" Nadine shouted. "He's done more than steal a car this time. He's murdered his father."

"You're hysterical, Mother. I don't know who killed Judge Bridges, but I do know that Dylan didn't." Maddie lowered her voice to a whisper as she grasped her mother's arm. "So will you, please, quiet down and stop voicing idiotic suppositions."

"Idiotic...?" Nadine sputtered. "I thought you'd wised up about men, but it seems you're as naive about that Bridges boy as you were when you were sixteen."

"As soon as Hart tells us it's all right to leave, I'm going to take you home," Maddie said. "It's been a trying night for all of us and I'm sure we should—"

Nadine glanced over Maddie's shoulder and gasped. "Oh, God."

"What is it?" Maddie turned around just in time to see the medics zipping Carl Bridges into a body bag. "Oh." She sought Dylan in the crowd and found him standing beside Justin Wainwright, who laid his hand on Dylan's shoulder and said something to him.

Knowing Justin as she did, she felt certain that whatever he'd said had been spoken with kindness.

An hour and a half later, Dylan drove off in his Porsche and the police told everyone that they could leave the country club. Hart walked over to where Joan waited with Maddie, each in turn soothing Nadine's overwrought nerves.

''Maddie, would you mind giving Joan a lift home?'' Hart asked. ''I'm going to head on down to the station.''

''Yes, I'd be glad to,'' Maddie replied, then reached out to grasp Hart's arm. ''Dylan Bridges might have been Mission Creek's rebel bad boy when he was sixteen, but he wasn't—and he isn't now—capable of murder. He'd come home to mend fences, to make things right with the judge. He was even considering moving back here to Mission Creek permanently.''

''And just how do you know so much about that man's personal plans?'' Nadine demanded.

Maddie ignored her mother. ''Hart, please, as a favor to me, do what you can to make things easier for Dylan when he's questioned. Remember, the man who was killed here tonight was Dylan's father.''

Hart patted Maddie's hand. ''If there's no evidence against Dylan Bridges, then there's no way we can hold him. And unless something shows up, I'd say he's in the clear.''

''Mark my word,'' Nadine said. ''That boy killed his daddy.''

"Mother!" Maddie turned on Nadine, her hands balled into tight fists. Take a deep breath and count to ten, Maddie ordered herself.

"Why don't y'all head on out now?" Hart said, then leaned over to kiss his wife. "Don't wait up. I'll probably be at the station all night."

As Maddie herded her mother and Joan toward the parking lot where her Mercedes Cabrio was parked, she said a silent prayer for Dylan. God help him and give him the comfort that no one else can.

"So, do I need to call a lawyer?" Dylan asked Chief Terry.

"You're not being charged with anything," the chief told him. "At this point, you aren't even a suspect. But since so many people seem to think you might have had a motive, I thought it best to ask you to come in and clarify a few things for us."

"Just what do you want clarified?"

"Mostly, we're curious about your relationship with your father. Why don't you go with Officer White and answer a few questions for him?"

"Yeah, sure."

Dylan followed the tall, broad-shouldered officer down the hall and into a quiet room.

"Have a seat," Officer White said.

Dylan sat.

"I'm Jake White, Mr. Bridges. I'm real sorry about

your father. Everyone who knew Judge Bridges liked and respected him.''

''Yeah. My dad was an all right guy.''

''We'll try not to keep you long. We just need to get some information.''

Jake White sat at the table directly across from Dylan. ''What sort of relationship did you have with your father?''

God help me, Dylan prayed. This has to be the worst nightmare of my life. Much worse than getting caught stealing Flynt Carson's Porsche. And even worse than spending two years in reform school. How was it possible that his father was dead? Who the hell would want to kill a good guy like his dad?

The reality of tonight's events played around the edges of Dylan's consciousness. His mind knew the facts. Someone had shot and killed his father. He'd seen his body floating in the pond at the country club. He'd watched while the medics took him away from the crime scene in a body bag. Took him to the morgue. But Dylan's heart refused to accept the facts. His dad couldn't be dead. Not now, not when they'd just found each other again after all these years. Four days wasn't nearly enough time together. Four lousy days being a real father and son. It wasn't fair that they'd been reunited only to be separated again. This time permanently.

''Mr. Bridges, did you understand the question?'' Jake asked.

Dylan nodded, then clenched his jaw in an effort to check his emotions. He blew out a long, got-to-get-control breath. "I hadn't seen my father in seventeen years. Not until four days ago. We had a falling-out when I was sixteen. I spent two years in the Reform Center for Boys in Amarillo for stealing a car, and when I got out at eighteen, I didn't come back to Mission Creek. Not until this week."

"And in all those years, you had no contact with Judge Bridges?"

Dylan shook his head. "My dad was a proud man, and it wasn't easy for him to admit when he was wrong. I guess I took after him in that way. I'm just as proud and stubborn."

"Why did you return to Mission Creek?"

"My father called me a little over a week ago. He'd hired a private detective to find me. He asked me to come for a visit. He wanted me to give him a second chance...give us a second chance."

The outer door opened and Hart O'Brien walked in, a cup of coffee in each hand. "You finished up here?" he asked Jake White.

"Not quite," Jake said.

Hart handed Dylan a cup filled with hot, black coffee. "Sorry about your father. Judge Bridges was a fine man."

Sensing a certain level of understanding coming from Detective O'Brien, Dylan said, "I didn't kill my father. Despite our past differences, I had no motive.

All I wanted was a chance to spend time with my dad, for us to rebuild our relationship.''

''I believe you,'' Hart said. ''But I am going to have to ask you not to leave town. Not for the time being.''

Dylan nodded, then took a sip of coffee. ''Like I told you at the country club, I'm not going anywhere, not until my father's murderer is found and brought to justice. And I can promise you something else, Detective. If the Mission Creek Police Department can't find the person responsible, I will.''

Maddie entered the living room of her condo. After dropping Joan off at her house, she'd deposited Nadine in Ernesta's loving care and escaped as quickly as possible. If she hadn't gotten away from her mother's endless tirade about her scandalous association with ''that Bridges boy,'' Maddie would have told her mother to go straight to hell.

God, what a night! Her nerves were frayed, her hands trembled, her stomach churned, and she felt as if she were going to start screaming any minute now. Get hold of yourself! Maddie Delarue doesn't fall apart; she stands strong against all odds.

Unzipping her gown as she made her way upstairs, Maddie recalled tonight's events—from the moment she caught a glimpse of a handsome stranger emerging from a sleek, black Porsche until the moment Dylan Bridges drove away in that same car, heading for the police station. She flipped on the overhead light as she entered her bedroom suite, a large, luxurious room that looked like something out of the pages of *House Beautiful.* A room like this was what an expensive San Antonio interior designer, with an unlimited budget, could create.

Maddie removed her three-inch black heels, then shucked off her one-of-a-kind satin gown. Walking around in her underwear, she went into the dressing room carrying the shoes and the dress. Methodically, she placed the shoes on the rack where they belonged and hung the dress on a padded hanger. Then she punched in a code on the security pad by the huge mirror on the back wall. The mirror was attached to a door, which swung open to reveal a wall safe. Maddie dialed the combination and opened the safe. She removed her earrings and bracelets, placed them in their velvet beds inside the safe, then closed first the safe door and then the mirrored door.

She slumped down on the large beige ottoman in the middle of the dressing room. Rope lighting behind the heavy molding spotlighted the vaulted ceiling. Her vision blurred as she stared upward, and her mind swirled with thoughts of Dylan Bridges.

Get that man out of your mind, she told herself. Maybe your mother is right—he's trouble with a capital T. Always has been, always will be. There was nothing she could do to help Dylan. She couldn't bring his father back to life. She couldn't erase the suspicions people had about him. All she could do was say another prayer for him and hope that he'd be all right.

Maddie removed her underwear, then rooted around in her closet until she found a thin cotton gown with spaghetti straps and lace on the bodice and hem. She walked into her enormous bathroom and busied herself with her nightly routine, ending with flossing and brushing her teeth.

Was Dylan still at the police station? she wondered. How long would they question him? Why couldn't they leave him alone? The poor man had just lost his father.

Memories of her father's death from a heart attack several years ago drifted through her mind. Was Dylan feeling now what she'd felt then? Losing a parent was one of the most difficult things a person ever faced in this life. And how much more tragic it was for Dylan because he'd missed so many years with his dad. Years that he could never get back. Thank God, she had reconciled with her father long before his death.

Maddie tossed the array of decorative pillows off her bed and onto the nearby beige damask easy chair, then she turned back the dusty lavender down comforter to reveal the dark gold sheets beneath. The elaborately carved Italian Renaissance four-poster dominated the elegant, austere bedchamber. After lying down, she punched the switch by her bed that turned off the lights, then she lay there quietly while her eyes adjusted to the darkness.

Perhaps tomorrow she should call Dylan. Just to offer her condolences. And perhaps she should ask him if he wanted her help in making the funeral arrangements. She'd been totally alone when she'd made arrangements for her father. Oh, there had been half a dozen lawyers and twice that many business associates at her beck and call, all of them offering her assistance. But her mother had been so upset when Jock Delarue died that the doctors had to keep her sedated for days. She'd attended the funeral at First Church in a drug-induced stupor. And Renee had been in such deep mourning over the loss of the man she loved that she'd gladly allowed Maddie to handle everything.

Tossing and turning, Maddie longed for sleep. But sleep wouldn't come. She fought her king-size pillows and rolled from one side of the enormous bed to the other. Count sheep, she told herself. Chant. Try to clear your mind of all thoughts. But that was easier said than done.

Minutes ticked by, slowly turning into several hours. Hugging one of her big pillows, Maddie lay curled in a semicircle, her knees drawn up to her chest. Still awake and unable to stop thinking about Dylan Bridges, she shot straight up in bed. One glance at the lighted digital clock on her nightstand told her it was two-thirty. Dammit, Maddie, just go ahead and do what you want to do, she told herself. She turned on the bedside lamp, got up and hurried into her dressing room. Rushing around as if time was of the essence, she dressed in jeans, a yellow blouse and a pair of yellow leather sandals.

Ten minutes later, Maddie drove through Mission Creek, a historic midsize town with a distinctive southwestern flair. She passed Mission Creek First Federal, the post office, the library and then the courthouse. She slowed her Mercedes as she eased up Royal Avenue, searching for 1010. There it was! A neat Craftsman house with a picket fence and age-old trees. She pulled her convertible up behind Dylan's Porsche, got out and walked to the front door.

Dylan Bridges, don't you dare try to send me away, she said to herself, as her index finger punched the doorbell.

Six

Dylan stood at the top of the stairs in his father's house and wondered who the hell was ringing the doorbell at this hour. He had left the police station less than thirty minutes ago and come straight home. Home? Yeah, it was odd how after all these years, this place still felt like home. Maybe he'd reverted into a kid, needing the safety of these four walls, this one particular house, to help him make sense of a world that suddenly had been turned upside down.

As he descended the stairs, he tried to stuff the tails of his white shirt back into his tuxedo slacks. Whoever was at the door had a really poor sense of timing. He wondered if the police decided they had enough circumstantial evidence to arrest him.

As he neared the front door, he glanced through the sheer curtain that covered the glass panes and saw the outline of a female form. His stomach knotted. It couldn't be her, could it? Why would Maddie Delarue be standing on the front porch of his father's home at—Dylan glanced again at his wristwatch—two-forty-eight in the morning?

He opened the door. Maddie looked at him, a sympathetic expression on her face and a hint of pleading in her big, blue eyes.

"Please, may I come in?" she asked.

He moved aside and with a sweep of his hand invited her into the small foyer. She moved past him, then paused to wait for him to close the door.

"Out kind of late, aren't you, Red?"

"I thought you might need some company," she replied. "I know under similar circumstances I wouldn't want to be alone."

"I'm used to being alone," he told her. "I'm a loner by nature. Always was. You should remember that."

Maddie nodded. "Loner or not, couldn't you use a friend?"

"Is that what you're here to offer me—friendship?"

"Condolences, friendship, tea and sympathy. Whatever you need."

"Right now I need a drink." He motioned toward the kitchen. "Want to join me? Somewhere the old man has a bottle of whiskey stashed for guests. In the kitchen cupboards, if I remember correctly. Dad wasn't much of a drinker. The expression 'sober as a judge' fit him to a T." Dylan's voice cracked with emotion.

When Maddie reached out to him, he moved quickly so that he was beyond her grasp, then he hurried into the kitchen. She followed directly behind him. He rummaged through the cupboards, ignoring her, until he found a three-quarters-full bottle of Crown Royal. Dylan figured this particular bottle was probably several years old. His dad had used liquor mainly for medicinal purposes, like to make hot toddies in the winter when he felt a cold coming on. After retrieving the bottle and two small juice glasses, Dylan turned back to Maddie.

"Have a seat." He indicated the chairs around the kitchen table.

After she took a seat, he sat across from her, placed the glasses on the table and opened the bottle. He poured himself a third of a glassful.

"Care to join me?" He held the open bottle over the second glass.

She shook her head. "No, thanks."

He set the bottle down, but left off the lid. As he lifted the glass to his mouth, he stared at Maddie. No makeup, face scrubbed, her shoulder-blade length red hair hanging in wild disarray, she was the prettiest thing he'd ever seen. And despite being thirty-three, she looked like a fresh-faced kid.

"Does your mama know where you are?" he asked, then took a hefty swig of whiskey. The liquor burned a hot trail on its way from his mouth to his stomach. He blew out a deep breath.

"You must have me confused with the sixteen-year-old Maddie," she said. "I don't answer to my mother. I haven't in a long time."

''Free and independent, huh? But surely you care what people might think if they knew you were aiding and abetting the notorious Dylan Bridges.''

''What happened at the police station?''

Dylan took another sip of whiskey. ''Why do you care?''

''Good question. Why do I care?'' She shrugged. ''For the life of me, I really don't know.'' She shoved back the chair, stood and glanced around the kitchen. ''Why don't I fix a pot of coffee and maybe scramble some eggs and make some toast? We could eat an early breakfast.''

Dylan chuckled. She stared at him questioningly.

''I'm not laughing at you,'' he said. ''It's just my mother's answer to most of life's problems was food. A cookie went with a skinned knee. A pot roast dinner would always soothe my dad after a rough day. You know, stuff like that. Tell me, do mothers teach their daughters that feeding men and children is the best way to give comfort?''

''I wouldn't know. My mother never so much as boiled an egg in her entire life.''

''But you know how to cook?'' He lifted his eyebrows in a skeptical expression. ''The richest gal in the state can actually scramble eggs?''

''It doesn't take a gourmet chef to scramble eggs.'' She rounded the table, laid her hand on Dylan's shoulder and smiled at him. ''I'll cook, we'll eat and you'll clean up the dishes. Deal?'' She held out her hand to him.

He rose from the chair, grasped her hand and replied, ''Deal.'' Who would have thought it? That Maddie would be standing in his dad's kitchen at three o'clock in the morning, offering to fix him breakfast.

Their gazes met and held. God, how was it possible, after everything that had happened, that all he wanted was to grab this woman and hold on to her for dear life? He didn't realize how tightly he was gripping her small hand until she tugged on it.

He released her hand immediately and noted the redness. ''God, Maddie, I'm sorry. I didn't mean to—''

''It's okay.'' She flapped her hand back and forth like a limp dishrag for a few seconds and grinned at him. ''The feeling is coming back now.'' She marched over to the refrigerator. ''Get me a mixing bowl, will you? And why don't you make the coffee?''

''Bossy, bossy,'' he kidded.

She removed an egg carton, milk and butter from the refrigerator. ''Talk to me, Dylan. You need to get it all out. Otherwise, you'll explode. Believe me, I know.'' She took a midsize ceramic bowl from him. ''When my father died, I tried to be very brave. I had to take care of all the arrangements and deal with not only my mother, but with my stepmother, too. About three weeks after my father's funeral, I fell apart. If it hadn't been for Joan—you met her tonight, Joan O'Brien—I don't know what I'd have done.''

What did she think he needed? A shoulder to cry on? Someone to hold his hand? If she believed that, then Maddie didn't know a damn thing about him. He didn't need anybody. He'd survived on his own for the past seventeen years and done just fine. He would do whatever had to be done—take care of the funeral arrangements, handle his father's affairs, make sure his dad's murderer was caught and punished—then he'd go back to Dallas and resume his life there.

''Look, Maddie, I appreciate your concern, but I don't need you to fix my breakfast or hold my hand or listen to me pour out my heart and soul.''

Maddie broke four eggs into the mixing bowl, added a little milk, then glanced over her shoulder while she beat the eggs into a light, fluffy concoction. ''Start the coffee, will you? And hand me some bread to pop into the toaster.'' She took down a skillet from the rack over the stove, sliced off a large dollop of butter, dumped it into the skillet and placed the skillet on the stove. ''So, are you going to tell me what happened at the police station?''

Dylan glared at her. Hadn't the woman heard a word he'd said? He'd all but told her that he didn't want her here, that he didn't need her. But of course that wasn't really true. He might not need her, but he sure as hell wanted her to stay. But you can't count on her, he reminded himself. He couldn't count on anybody except himself. If he'd learned anything in life, he had learned that lesson the hard way.

"Are you surprised they didn't throw me in jail?" he asked, his voice tinged with sarcasm.

She poured the whipped eggs into the skillet. "The police have no evidence against you, so there's no reason for them to have arrested you."

Dylan spooned ground coffee from the can into the filter, then added water and turned on the coffeemaker. "They have absolutely no idea who killed my dad. I'm the only one who seems to have been at odds with the judge, so they're going to check me out thoroughly. I just hate to see them wasting time that way, when they need to be figuring out who had a reason to murder my father."

When Dylan removed a loaf of bread from the bread box on the counter, Maddie turned the heat down on the skillet, then took the bread from him and placed four slices in the toaster.

"Do you suspect anyone?" she asked. "I don't suppose Judge Bridges told you he had an enemy who might want to do him harm, did he?"

Dylan shook his head. "What are you doing, Maddie, trying to play amateur detective?"

"Just thinking out loud."

"Well, I've been back in Mission Creek only four days, so I don't know everything that was going on in Dad's life, but I do know that something was bothering him. He ate antacids like they were candy and every time the phone rang, he tensed.''

''Did you ask him why—''

''I asked. He said it was nothing for me to worry about. Now, I'm wondering if he'd really picked up a virus of some sort and didn't feel up to going to the Mystery Gala last night or if he backed out for a different reason.''

''Like what?'' The toast popped up. Maddie buttered the slices and placed them on a plate, then spooned the eggs on to two waiting plates. ''Judge Bridges had a reputation for being as honest as the day is long, so he wouldn't have been involved in anything illegal. What does that leave?''

''It leaves him knowing about something illegal going on and he was about to blow the whistle. Somebody could have killed him to stop him from exposing them.''

Maddie carried the plates to the table, then added silverware. ''That scenario makes sense to me. And surely the police will look into all the criminal cases that were on the judge's docket.''

Dylan poured their coffee and set two steaming mugs beside their plates. ''If they do it right, they'll consider every possibility.'' He pulled out a chair, sat and looked at the scrambled eggs. ''Smells good.'' He tasted them. ''So you can cook.''

''Told you I could.'' Maddie joined him at the table. ''So, what do you think some other possibilities might be?''

''Maybe somebody was blackmailing Dad, or it's possible he was in possession of information someone wanted. And it could be that a criminal he put away got out and came after him. Considering Dad's line of work, the possibilities are endless.''

''Were you aware that you father was the defense attorney in a very high profile case some years ago?'' Maddie sipped on her coffee.

''Afraid not. Unless it hit the front pages in Dallas, I wouldn't have known about it. So, who was involved?''

''Haley Mercado drowned in a boating accident.'' Maddie played with her eggs, scooting them around on the plate with her fork.

''Mercado? I remember a Ricky Mercado. Came from a suspected mob family.''

''Haley was the younger sister. She went partying with some local heroes from the 14th Marines and somehow ended up drowning. Her body was found and identified and her family brought charges against Luke Callaghan, Flynt Carson, Spence Harrison and Tyler Murdoch.''

''Hmm. Rich, powerful families involved, huh?''

''Your father defended them and got them off. Rumor was that the Mercado family and Haley's former fiancé were less than pleased.''

''But that was a few years ago?'' Dylan asked.

Maddie nodded as she munched on a slice of buttered toast.

"If it was revenge, why wait that long?" Dylan rubbed the back of his neck. "Damn! I feel like such a bastard. Here my father is dead, killed by some unknown person, and you know more about what's been going on in his life these past seventeen years than I do—his own son."

"Don't beat yourself up over what can't be changed. Concentrate on the fact that you and your father had reconciled, that you at least had these past few days together."

"Yeah, four lousy days." Dylan scooted back his chair, stood and walked toward the door. "If I'd swallowed my pride and come home a few years ago—hell, a few months ago—maybe I could have done something to have prevented this. Maybe my father would have trusted me enough to have confided in me."

Maddie got up and walked over to where Dylan gazed through the glass panes in the back door, then placed her hand on his shoulder. "I'm sure that eventually he would have told you what was bothering him. He probably didn't want to ruin your first few days together."

Dylan shrugged off Maddie's hand, opened the door and walked out onto the back porch. The quiet hum of early morning, a few hours before dawn, whispered softly in the darkness. Maddie followed him outside, where, her hand linked with his, they stood on the porch and gazed up at the night sky. They were silent and unmoving. Dylan could hear only their steady breathing.

"If you're smart, you'll get the hell away from me," Dylan said, his calm voice belying the anger of his words. "I'm a total failure when it comes to personal relationships...even friendships. Hang around long enough and I'm bound to hurt you."

"You stole my line, you know. I'm the one who had two fiancés and numerous admirers, but not even one real love affair." Maddie squeezed his hand. "You shouldn't go through these next few days alone. Making the funeral arrangements will be more difficult than you can imagine. And then there will be the funeral itself and dealing with all the people who'll pay their condolences."

"I doubt the folks in Mission Creek will pay their condolences to me. Half the people at the country club last night probably believe I killed my father." Dylan yanked his hand from hers, went down the porch steps and into the backyard.

Why was she still here? Why hadn't she deserted him, run off and left him high and dry the way she'd done when they'd been sixteen and he'd gotten them into trouble? What the hell did Maddie want with a guy who couldn't cause her anything but misery?

When he felt her gentle touch on his shoulder, he jerked around and glared at her. Damn, he wished she'd stop looking at him that way. As if she wanted nothing more than to wrap her arms around him and kiss away his blues.

Don't do it, he told himself. Don't take what she's offering. Don't use her to get through these next few hours. She deserves better.

Unable to resist, he surrendered to his baser instincts, pulled Maddie into his arms and kissed her with a savage, uncontrollable hunger that made her shudder. He wanted to absorb her into him, take her comfort and concern and wrap himself it in, cocoon himself from reality with her sweet body. She opened up to him, totally giving, allowing him to possess her almost brutally. He wanted her. Here and now. In the backyard, in the cool darkness. As he ended the kiss, he pressed his cheek against hers, then cupped her buttocks with his hands and lifted her up and into his erection.

"Don't you see how it is with me?" he moaned against her ear. "I don't play by the rules. That's why I'm so successful. Hang around, honey, and I'll make you sorry that you ever knew me."

"Dylan, please..."

He grabbed her shoulders, stared at her beautiful face, softly visible by moonlight, and centered his gaze on her trusting blue eyes. "Get the hell away from me. For your own self-preservation." He shoved her away.

Maddie staggered momentarily, but managed to balance herself. "Dylan Bridges, you are the most aggravating man I've ever known. What's wrong with you that you can't accept a little human comfort and a genuine offer of help?"

"Why do you want to help me? You don't have a dog in this race, Red, so why stick around?"

"Oh!" Maddie growled the word. "You numbskull! I happen to like you. I liked you when we were kids and I like you now. And I respected Judge Bridges a great deal. Isn't that reason enough?" She paused, but he didn't respond. "If it isn't, then consider this—your father was murdered at the country club, during a party that I planned and executed. So you could say that the judge was killed on my territory, on my watch, and I'd like to help you in any way I can. And that help even includes assisting you in your search for your father's killer."

"Are you offering to help me play amateur sleuth?" Shaking his head, he snorted. "Spoiled, pampered Maddie Delarue would actually get her hands dirty playing detective?"

"If you think your insults will scare me off, then think again," she told him. "I know what you're trying to do and it won't work."

"What am I trying to do?"

"You want to make me so angry I'll leave you alone. Isn't that it? In the past, everyone in your life deserted you when you needed them most. First your mother died just as you were changing from a boy into a young man, then I didn't stand by you when you got arrested for stealing that car, and after that your father didn't do anything to help keep you out of boys' reform school. Have there been others who have disappointed you, too?"

Dylan didn't speak, only stood there staring at her. The silence between them grew louder and louder with each passing moment.

"I'll stand beside you this time, Dylan, if you'll give me the chance."

He cleared his throat. "Yeah, okay. Fine with me. If you want to help me, want to play Nora to my Nick Charles, then I'll see you tomorrow—make that later today—and we can decide where to start."

"Thanks, Dylan." She stood on tiptoe, kissed his cheek and said, "I'm very sorry about your dad."

Maddie turned and walked away, through the back gate and around the house. Dylan stood in that one spot until she was out of sight, then he inhaled and exhaled deeply. After a few minutes of useless pondering about his feelings for Maddie, he went over and sat down on the porch steps.

I'll stand by you this time, Dylan. Her words repeated themselves over and over in his mind. He wanted to believe her, but did he dare? Could he trust her not to desert him if things got nasty? How would she react if people pointed fingers at him and called him a murderer?

He knew one thing for sure: With or without Maddie Delarue's help, he intended to prove his innocence beyond any doubt. And if the police couldn't find his father's killer, he would.

When Molly French Gates came on duty later that morning, Hart O'Brien filled her in on the previous night's events at the country club. Molly had been part of the task force that had exposed the corrupt cops in the police department back in March, and Hart respected her greatly.

"It's all over the news," Molly said. "In the *Clarion,* on TV. They're saying y'all brought Dylan Bridges in for questioning. Is that true? Does the department actually consider the judge's son a suspect?"

Hart took a sip of his strong, lukewarm coffee, then rubbed his hand over his face. "Not as far as I'm concerned. The guy seemed totally shocked by his father's death. And just being estranged from his old man isn't enough motive for murder. Besides, we could be looking at a sloppy professional hit. Not some polished wise guy from out of state. Maybe a local hood."

"The judge pissed off the wrong person, huh? Is that your take?"

Hart yawned. "Something like that."

Molly slapped Hart on the back. "Why don't you go on home? You look as if you're dead on your feet. I wouldn't want to have to call Joan to come get you."

Hart chuckled. "You know, there's one thing that

puzzles me. If this was a professional hit, even a sloppy one, then why the hell did the guy do something as stupid as leaving the murder weapon in the pond, not five feet from Carl Bridges' body?''

''Are you sure it's the murder weapon?''

''Pretty sure. The ballistics report will verify it.''

''And what about fingerprints on the gun?''

''We should get so lucky.''

Using a phony ID, he'd checked into a motel outside of town last night. And he had slept like a baby. Odd how taking a guy out always had that effect on him. Kind of like getting laid. Yeah, almost as good; sometimes even better.

He'd planned everything, down to the last detail, learning the layout of the country club and where each employee would be at any given time. The valets for the gala kept out of sight, in the private parking area, fraternizing with the chauffeurs during the party. The only problem was that Judge Bridges hadn't shown up as expected. But a phone call to the old man threatening his son's life had gotten him down to the club pretty quick.

He'd given the judge one final chance to come clean, to give him the information he wanted—the info his boss demanded. But the stupid old man had refused to talk. Hell, hadn't he known who he was dealing with? The boss didn't take no for an answer. His orders had been to find out the information or else.

The hit had gone off perfectly until that damn stupid redheaded waitress came outside for a smoke. How the hell was he supposed to know she'd come out to the front of the club instead of the back where he'd been told the staff took their smoke breaks? And what the hell had possessed her to walk so far down the driveway? If he'd hung around a second longer, she might have seen him. As it was, he just barely got away. But when she startled him, he accidentally dropped his 9mm Sig and it fell over into the pond. He'd tried his damnedest to recover the gun, but it had come down to choosing whether to retrieve the Sig or risk getting caught by the waitress. Leaving behind the murder weapon had been the least risky of his two choices. But the cops wouldn't find any fingerprints on his weapon. He always coated his fingertips with glue before a hit. That way he never left fingerprints on anything.

He'd called the boss and left the message they'd agreed on. ''Justice has been served.'' The boss had a sense of humor.

His stomach growled. Damn, he was hungry. He could eat a horse this morning. But maybe he'd just stop by the Mission Creek Café for a big helping of steak and eggs, and while he ate breakfast, he'd take a look at the *Clarion* and see what the local reporters were saying about Judge Bridges' murder at the country club last night.

Seven

Wearing dark sunglasses to hide the puffiness under her eyes, Maddie arrived at the country club two hours late. After leaving Dylan early this morning, she'd fallen asleep the minute she returned home and laid down on her bed fully clothed. During her brief nap she had dreamed. They'd been those silly, confusing kind of dreams where nothing made sense. But on awakening, she remembered one main theme in them—Dylan Bridges was a part of her life now and there was no escaping that fact.

Dylan was a man alone, with no one to stand by him and help him. And for some inexplicable reason Maddie longed to be that person, the strong, dependable friend he could lean on. Dylan was a complicated man, one who didn't trust easily or accept help readily. Breaking through his protective shield would be a challenge—probably the biggest challenge of Maddie's life. Strange how she now relished a challenge, when as a teenager she'd shied away from challenges and confrontations of any kind.

What made her willing to risk getting hurt, having her heart broken again, just to help a man who had tried to send her away? Maybe because she felt that Dylan and she were two of a kind. Neither trusted easily, both had been hurt and disappointed by life and love, and they were both so terribly alone.

"Morning, Maddie." As she walked into the outer office suite, Alicia handed her a cup of hot tea. "I've been fielding calls for you and there are at least two dozen messages waiting for you on your desk. I've been telling people that you're in a meeting. I hope that was all right."

Alicia followed Maddie into her private office. "Yes, Alicia, thank you." Maddie dumped her handbag on her desk, set the cup on the coaster to the right of her computer screen and glared at the stack of bright yellow message slips neatly stacked in the square plastic box she used for that purpose. Maddie had always prided herself on being highly organized.

"Your mother has phoned every thirty minutes since nine o'clock." Alicia glanced sympathetically at Maddie. "I didn't write down any of her messages."

Maddie groaned. "Next time she calls put her through. If I don't talk to her, she'll come over here, and I simply cannot deal with Nadine in person this morning."

Alicia nodded. "Mr. Small has been asking where you are. He needs to speak to you. But I can tell you what he's going to say."

"Good. You tell me and then when Harvey shows up, I can get rid of him quickly. That little toad has never been one of my favorite people, and after last night he's in the top five on my people-I-detest list.''

''I'm sure you noticed all the law enforcement people milling around inside and out.'' Alicia waited for Maddie to nod before she continued. ''Well, the club is closed today...because of the murder last night. But the temporary grill will be open for the employees. That's one of the things Harvey wanted to tell you. And the other is that we're to cooperate fully with the police department and the sheriff's department. It seems Sheriff Wainwright and Chief Terry have joined forces on this one. Killing a circuit judge is pretty much the same as killing a police officer.''

Maddie sat in her comfortable chair, lifted her cup and sipped the hot peppermint tea. Lack of sleep combined with tension had given Maddie a throbbing headache and even though she'd taken a couple of aspirin before leaving her condo, the ache had dulled only slightly.

''I'll be eating lunch here at my desk today,'' Maddie said. ''But I'll take care of ordering something from the grill. And please continue fielding my calls. I don't want to speak to anyone, unless it's absolutely necessary. The only exceptions are my mother and...Dylan Bridges.''

''Dylan Bridges?'' Alicia's eyes rounded in surprise. ''Isn't he a suspect in the judge's murder?''

Maddie sighed, removed her sunglasses and glared pointedly at her assistant. ''No. He is not a suspect.''

"But I thought Mr. Small said that—"

"Harvey Small is an idiot!"

Someone cleared their throat. Not Maddie or Alicia. Maddie glanced past her assistant to the open doorway. There stood Harvey. Oh, great, Maddie thought. Just what I need.

"Good morning, Ms. Delarue." Harvey marched into her office. "Thanks so much for finally showing up for work this morning. We all had a difficult night, but some of us were able to arrive on time for work today."

"Stuff it, Harvey," Maddie snapped.

"I resent your attitude," he replied.

"And I resent you. So, we're even."

Harvey pursed his lips. His round, fat face turned red. "If you weren't who you are, there's no way you would keep your job."

Maddie burst into laughter. When Harvey's rotund body tensed, he looked as if he were about to explode.

Harvey puffed out his chest and tilted his chin. "You might have me fired for what I'm about to say, but it's obvious to everyone that Dylan Bridges probably murdered his father and he tried to use you as an alibi. If you weren't involved with the man, you wouldn't be defending him."

Maddie narrowed her gaze, looked point-blank at Harvey and said, "The only reason I haven't gotten rid of you before now is because, despite your unpleasant personality, you're damn good at your job.

But remember one thing, little man—you can be replaced.''

Snorting, his face red as a beet, Harvey turned and practically ran out of Maddie's office.

Alicia released a long, pent-up breath and then giggled. ''I thought he was going to explode.''

''That would have been a sight worth paying to see.''

''Ms. Delarue?''

''Yes?''

''The police asked me a lot of questions about your whereabouts last night. They seem very curious about your having been with Mr. Bridges. I told them what time you arrived back at the party last night. I hope I didn't say—''

Maddie held up a restraining hand. ''It's all right. We've all got to tell the truth. I was with Dylan, except for about fifteen minutes, and that's exactly what I told the police last night.''

''Yes, ma'am.''

The ringing telephone prompted Alicia's hasty departure. When she rushed back to her desk, Maddie closed her eyes and huffed out a tired breath. She had a feeling this was going to be a very long day.

Alicia stuck her head in the door. ''It's your mother.''

Maddie groaned.

A uniformed policeman met Dylan at the entrance to the country club. ''Sorry, sir, but the club is closed today. There was a murder here last night and—''

"Yes, I know. My father was the victim."

The young officer blushed and stammered, "You're...er...you're Dylan Bridges? Sorry about... The judge was a fine man."

"Yes, he was." Dylan glanced around, taking note of the small swarm of law enforcement personnel present at the club this morning. "I'm not here as a club member. I'm here to see Ms. Delarue."

"Is Ms. Delarue expecting you?"

"Yes, I believe she is," Dylan replied.

The policeman opened the door and held it for Dylan.

"Thank you."

The officer nodded.

Once inside, Dylan hesitated momentarily, wondering just where Maddie's office was located. A couple of staff members milling around in the lobby apparently recognized him. They stared at him, then whispered among themselves. What were they saying? Were they taking odds on whether or not he killed his father? Damn, what a predicament to be in—mourning a parent's death and having to defend himself against untrue accusations all at the same time. Ignore those people, he told himself. He would have to get used to being stared at, whispered about and suspected.

Okay, all he had to do was remember where the offices were seventeen years ago when he'd worked here as a valet. The memory clicked into place instantly and he took the elevator to the second floor, which he assumed still housed the office space, as well as the guest rooms. A few minutes later he stood outside the closed door with an attached plaque proclaiming the suite within was the private domain of Ms. Delarue, Events Manager. When he opened the door, a wide-eyed, gaping-mouthed young woman nervously stood up behind her desk.

"Mr. Bridges...good morning, sir."

Dylan offered her a smile. "I'd like to see Maddie, please."

"Uh...yes, sir. Just a moment and I'll let her know that you're here."

Dylan waited while the girl disappeared into Maddie's office. She returned instantly, leaving the door open behind her.

"Please, go right in."

"Thanks."

Dylan entered Maddie's office and closed the door behind him. Maddie rose from her desk and came forward, her hand outstretched. He took a good look at her and from the dark, puffy circles under her eyes realized she'd probably gotten no more sleep than he had. But she was beautiful, with her hair neatly secured in a loose bun, and wearing a stylish beige suit.

She motioned to the chairs in front of her desk. "Won't you sit down?"

He shook his head. "I won't be here long. I just

wanted to stop by to say thanks for the scrambled eggs this morning. And I wanted to tell you that I've made tentative funeral arrangements. All we need is the date. I'll have to wait until the coroner releases his body. They'll have to do an autopsy, of course.''

When Dylan winced at the thought of his father's body being opened up like some damn lab experiment, Maddie reached out and squeezed his arm. He looked at her. Sweet Maddie. Genuinely concerned, warmly caring.

Clearing his throat, Dylan asked, ''So, Red, have you come to your senses? Are you thinking a little clearer now than you were at three this morning?''

She released his arm. ''Meaning, I suppose, have I decided to steer clear of you?''

He didn't know why her response was so damn important to him. After all, he'd told her to get lost, hadn't he? He didn't want her to wind up getting hurt by associating with him. But all the logical reasoning in the world didn't change one irrefutable fact—the sixteen-year-old kid part of him wanted Maddie Delarue to stand by his side.

Maddie eased back, leaned her hips against the edge of her desk and stared at him. He had showered and shaved and changed clothes, but he suspected the haggard expression on his face plainly revealed the hell he'd been through during the past twelve hours.

''I can't quite figure you out,'' Maddie said. ''It's

as if you're pushing me away with one hand and dragging me closer with the other.''

He grinned. ''Yeah, I guess my actions are rather confusing. Believe me, I'm as confused as you are.''

''Why don't we clear up the confusion?'' Maddie crossed her arms over her chest. ''I haven't changed my mind about anything. I want to help you, stand by your side, work with you. But it'll be a lot easier for both of us if you stop resisting me.''

''Is that what I've been doing?''

''Sit down, will you?'' She motioned to the chairs again. ''I'm going to order lunch for myself and I'd like for you to join me. I don't think either of us ate much of those scrambled eggs this morning. So, what will it be, sandwich and chips or a salad?''

Dylan took the chair to Maddie's front left, lifted his leg and crossed it over the other at the knee. ''Ham and cheese sandwich.'' Only a few nights ago, his dad had prepared him a ham and cheese sandwich. Emotion lodged in Dylan's throat. He'd been so pleased that his father had actually remembered his preferences.

Maddie pivoted halfway around on her desk, lifted the telephone, tapped in a number and said, ''This is Ms. Delarue. I'd like to place a lunch order and I want it delivered to my office.''

While Maddie ordered lunch, Dylan watched her, noting numerous little things about her. The way she tilted her head to one side, how she narrowed her gaze when she concentrated, the way she unconsciously gnawed on her bottom lip when she was impatient.

Placing the receiver back on the hook, Maddie huffed. "That poor girl must be a new employee. She seemed rattled. But I have every hope that we'll get what I ordered."

Dylan nodded. "By the way, I stopped by the police station this morning."

Maddie focused on him. "You did?"

"Yeah, I talked to Chief Terry. Caught up with him just as he was heading home. He told me that they'd found what they believe is the murder weapon. It seems the killer might have dropped it in the pond where my dad's body was found."

Maddie raised her eyebrows. "That was rather careless, wasn't it?"

Dylan shrugged. "Could've been carelessness. Or maybe the gun was a plant. Or possibly someone startled the killer and he lost the gun and didn't have time to retrieve it. There are several possibilities."

"Did the chief tell you whether or not anyone has come forward to say they saw what happened or—"

"No witnesses," Dylan said. "But that waitress, Erica Clawson, might have seen something and just doesn't realize it. After all, the authorities believe she discovered my dad's body shortly after he'd been shot."

"Mmm-hmm. So, I assume the gun is being tested

for fingerprints and all that other stuff...ballistics or whatever.''

''Yeah, but I was told that it's rare fingerprints are found on a weapon. Guess that would make it too easy to solve this crime.'' Dylan leaned over, dropped his hands between his spread thighs and tapped the tips of his fingers together. ''Fingerprints would prove conclusively that I didn't fire the weapon.''

''You aren't really a suspect. If you were, they would have held you last night.''

''They did tell me not to leave town.'' Shaking his head, Dylan grimaced. ''As if I'd leave before I saw my father's killer brought to justice.''

''Have you contacted a lawyer? If you need a recommendation, I'd be glad to—''

''I called my lawyer in Dallas first thing this morning. And I made arrangements with my partners in our brokerage firm to handle all my obligations for the time being.''

''Then you've covered all your bases.''

''I think so.'' Dylan lifted his gaze to Maddie's face. ''I imagine the police have already asked—or if they haven't, they will—but I'd like to see the guest list for last night's Mystery Gala. Would that be possible?''

Maddie's expression sobered instantly. He noted a slight tension in her shoulders and a tightening in her jaw. ''They haven't requested the list, but you're right, I'm sure they will.''

"Would you get in trouble if you let me take a look at the list?"

"I don't know." Maddie eased up, went around her desk and sat, then placed her hands at the keyboard and began typing. "If you want to see it, here it is." She motioned for him to come to her.

Dylan released a relieved sigh. He hadn't been sure Maddie would cooperate. He rounded her desk and stood behind her. Together they scanned the list of party attendees.

"All the movers and shakers in Mission Creek," Dylan said. "Do you see anyone on that list who might have had reason to want my father dead?"

Maddie studied the names, putting faces and personal connections to each name. She knew these people. Some were friends; all were acquaintances. "All of these people knew your father and many were personal friends. I can't imagine anyone on this list being capable of murder. As a matter of fact, other than some of the criminals your father has sentenced, I can't think of anyone, except maybe the Mercado family, who might have had a grudge against Judge Bridges."

"That's something that has me confused. I was too out of it to wonder this morning when you first told me about Dad taking on a case, but since my father was a circuit judge, how was it possible for him to take on a case as a defense lawyer?"

"Didn't he tell you that a few years ago he thought

he wanted to retire, so he didn't run for reelection? During that time, he taught some college classes and I believe he started writing a book. He defended the men charged with Haley Mercado's murder while he was campaigning for reelection. Actually after winning that case, he was a shoo-in. With both the Wainwrights and the Carsons backing him, how could he have lost?''

''There's still so much I don't know about my father's life. Things I should know.''

Just as Maddie lifted her hand and placed it on Dylan's arm, Alicia knocked on the door, then opened it and said, ''Your lunch is here. Do you want the waitress to bring it in?''

''Wonderful,'' Maddie said. ''Yes, please, send her in.'' Dylan stepped aside while Maddie cleared off a space on her desk.

The waitress entered with a large tray that held their lunch orders. ''Where would you like this? On your desk?''

''Right here.'' Maddie tapped the spot.

The waitress set down the tray, then glanced at Dylan. ''You're Judge Bridges' son, aren't you?''

Dylan nodded. For a split second he wondered if this young woman was going to lambaste him for killing his father. But her warm smile reassured him that she wasn't.

''I'm very sorry about your father,'' she said. ''He seemed like a really nice man. He was one of my favorite customers here at the club. He was always so friendly and...a very generous tipper.''

''Thank you, Miss...''

''Parker. Daisy Parker.'' The waitress smiled shyly, then bowed her head and left hurriedly.

When Daisy closed the door behind her, Maddie said, ''Let's eat.''

Dylan pulled up a chair to the desk and sat. They ate in relative silence. Then while they sipped on their colas and nibbled on the huge chocolate chip cookies Maddie had ordered for dessert, they discussed possibilities and narrowed their personal suspects list down to the Mercado family, particularly reputed mob boss Carmine Mercado and Haley's ex-fiancé, Frank Del Brio, who Maddie told Dylan was reportedly the first in line to succeed Carmine.

''Unless we find out that someone Dad sentenced to prison had a grudge against him, then we don't have much else to go on. Maybe Carmine or the Del Brio guy wanted to punish my father for getting off the men they believed killed Haley.''

''You do realize that you're talking about poking your nose into the mob, don't you?'' Maddie shuddered. ''I hear those people are bad news.''

''What about the local authorities? What's your take on their willingness to investigate the mob?''

''The mob had a stranglehold on the local police, but the department cleaned house a few months ago,'' Maddie explained. ''As far as I know, Burl Terry is a straight-arrow kind of guy. And I know for a fact that Justin Wainwright isn't intimidated by anyone, mob connected or not."

"If my father's murder was a professional hit, then tracking down the killer could get really nasty." Dylan looked directly at Maddie. "Are you sure you want to—"

"I'm in this with you to the end," she told him.

"Why?"

"Why? I—I'm not sure. Let's just say that I've learned how to be a better friend than I was when I was sixteen."

"Is that all there is to it—friendship?" Dylan stood.

Maddie swallowed. "Friendship and..." Dylan rounded the desk, reached down and lifted her out of her chair.

"And?"

"And you and I are a lot alike. I think I understand you, Dylan Bridges. Besides, I've had the hots for you since I was a teenager," she admitted, the words rushing out on one long breath. "Not very smart of me, I admit. But it's the truth."

Damn! Of all the things he'd been expecting her to say, this wasn't it. Maddie had just told him that she had the hots for him. Hell, didn't she realize that he wanted her so much that he'd do just about anything to get her in his bed?

"I have no doubt that you'd be very good for me." He pulled her into his arms. "The problem is, Maddie,

I wouldn't be good for you. My life is all messed up right now. I've taken a leave of absence from work and left behind a life I thought was just great, but now I'm beginning to realize I was missing a great deal. My father has been murdered, and I'm embarking on my own personal crusade to find his killer and nail the guy's ass to the barn wall. You don't want to go along for this ride with me."

Maddie draped her arms around his neck. "Yes, I do."

"You're crazy. You know that, don't you?"

"I know that you need at least one friend right now," Maddie said, "one person on your side."

"And you're that person."

"If you'll let me be."

"I know I shouldn't." Dylan lowered his head until his lips were almost touching hers. "But, yeah, I could use a friend right about now."

He kissed her. A strong, vital kiss that could easily have deepened and progressed to a more intimate level had someone not knocked on Maddie's office door.

"Damn," Dylan cursed under his breath.

They broke apart as if they were guilty of a crime.

"Yes?" Maddie asked.

Alicia opened the door. "Detective O'Brien is here. He wants to take a look at the guest list for last night's Mystery Gala."

Eight

Five days after his death, Carl Bridges' funeral was held at First Church, and it seemed that half the population of Mission Creek was either inside the building or outside lined up down the sidewalk. The church was filled to overflowing with floral arrangements. If Dylan hadn't already been well aware of the fact that his father was one of the most highly respected citizens of this town, today's turnout would have proven it to him.

Dylan wasn't sure how he would have gotten through these past few days without Maddie Delarue. He'd finally given up in his halfhearted attempts to warn her off. Despite her uncanny ability to see through his I-don't-need-anybody facade and despite the way she'd already gotten under his skin, he found he really didn't want to send her away. But his cautious nature warned him that she was in his life on a temporary basis, so he shouldn't get used to having her around.

They'd had dinner together every night at her condo, spending time getting to know each other while going over all the information they'd been able to gather about his father's death and about his life during the past few years. The police had come up with very little, except that the ballistics report proved the bullets that killed Carl had indeed come from the gun found in the pond. A Sig Model P230. A stainless steel, twenty ounce 9mm that held seven rounds. Three had been fired into his father's chest. There were no fingerprints on the gun, which wasn't a surprise to anyone. A check on the weapon showed it belonged to a guy named Tom Smith from Laredo, who'd reported the Sig stolen from his Jeep two weeks ago. Smith was an upstanding citizen with no record. Another dead end.

Dylan stood to the side of his father's casket. Alone in a church filled with people, he tried to remain in control of his emotions as mourners descended on him, each person respectfully sympathetic when they spoke to him about his father. But he could see doubt and suspicion in several sets of eyes. People wondering if he was the murderer. Of course no one implied verbally what they were thinking. If ever he needed a shoulder to lean on, today was the day. He had no family, other than some distant cousins he didn't even know. His father had been an only child and his mother's only sibling, an older brother, had been killed in Vietnam back in the late sixties.

Dylan caught a whiff of Maddie's expensive floral perfume, a scent he'd grown accustomed to this past week. While shaking hands with one of his father's lawyer cronies, he glanced over the man's shoulder and saw Maddie only a few feet away. She was regal and serene in her stylish black suit, tiny black hat and with black pearl earrings shimmering against her white earlobes. She hurried around the line of people waiting to view the deceased and came up beside Dylan.

"I'm sorry I wasn't here sooner." She stood on tiptoe and whispered in his ear. "I had a minor emergency with Mother."

"Is she all right?" he asked.

Maddie blew out an exasperated breath. "She's fine. Nothing to worry about."

"She didn't want you to be here with me today, did she?"

"I've told you—I'm my own person," Maddie said. "My mother doesn't run my life. She doesn't make my decisions for me."

Dylan shook hands with and spoke to several people, each of whom eyed Maddie with surprise that quickly turned to speculation. God only knew what these good people would say behind Maddie's back.

"If you stay at my side today, what do you suppose people will think?" he asked.

"You know what?" Again, she lowered her voice to a whisper. "I don't give a damn."

A great sense of appreciation swelled up inside Dylan. After today, he'd owe Maddie more than he could ever repay. Seventeen years ago, when they'd been kids, she'd let him down and disappointed him in the worst way. But she had more than made up for the past. Today she'd tipped the scales.

Dylan recognized one of the two young women coming forward in the line. He couldn't remember the blonde's name, but she'd delivered lunch to Maddie's office the morning after his father's murder. She'd told him what a nice man his dad had been. The auburn-haired woman who was with her looked quite young, probably no more than twenty.

Maddie shook hands with both women. "Thank y'all for coming today." She turned to Dylan. "This is Daisy Parker and Ginger Walton, two of our country club employees."

"We're so sorry about Judge Bridges," Ginger said. "Everybody who worked at the club liked him."

As the minutes ticked by, the line of mourners began to seem endless. Maddie stood by Dylan as the line proceeded slowly to and then past him. Finally the bell tower struck the hour. Two o'clock. Time for the service to officially start. Maddie sat with him, holding his hand, right there in front of God and the entire assembly. The minister praised Carl Bridges as a man, as a judge, as a human being and as a fine Christian. He offered his condolences to Dylan and then asked the congregation to bow their heads in prayer. Somehow Dylan managed not to fall apart, at least not visibly. Inside he was dying.

Ford Carson gave the eulogy. When he said, "Carl

loved his son dearly and I know that his fondest wish was to be reunited with Dylan,'' emotion lodged in Dylan's throat and unshed tears gathered in the corners of his eyes.

When soft murmurs rose from the crowd, Maddie squeezed Dylan's hand. He sensed her silent message. I believe in you. Together, we can get through this day. At least that was what he hoped and prayed she was telling him. Odd how that for a man who hadn't needed anybody in a long, long time, he suddenly found himself growing dependent on Maddie. God help him.

During the brief ceremony at the graveside, an army reserve unit gave a twenty-one-gun salute, then presented Dylan with an American flag. Bagpipers, brought in from San Antonio on Delarue, Inc.'s private jet, played the mournful ''Amazing Grace.'' Overhead the afternoon sun beamed brightly. Not a cloud in the sky. Even the weather paid tribute to Carl Bridges.

When the service ended, Dylan escorted Maddie toward the waiting limousine. Leaving his wife's side, Hart O'Brien caught up with Dylan and called out his name.

Dylan stopped and turned. While the small crowd that had assembled at the graveside dispersed, Hart said, ''We need to talk.''

''Here?'' Dylan asked.

''How about inside the limo? That would give us some privacy.''

''What's this all about?'' Maddie inquired.

Hart motioned toward the open limousine door. Dylan waited for Maddie to slip inside, then followed her. Hart got in, closed the door and sat opposite them.

''I'm going by my gut instincts,'' Hart said. ''And by the fact that my wife says that if Maddie believes in you, then you're an okay guy.'' A hint of a smile played at the corners of Hart's mouth. ''I know you've been snooping around, asking questions. You need to let us, the police, handle things. You could get in over your head—'' he glanced at Maddie ''—and take Maddie with you, straight into some big trouble.''

''Y'all find my father's killer and I'll back off,'' Dylan said. ''Until then—''

''What if I keep you informed?'' Hart asked. ''What if you know what we know—would that satisfy you? Would you stop playing amateur detective then?''

''Are you making the offer?'' Dylan looked Hart square in the eyes.

''I got an okay from Chief Terry to keep you posted,'' Hart said.

''I'm no longer a suspect?''

''Not as far as the police are concerned.''

Dylan understood his meaning. The police had no real reason to suspect Dylan and no evidence of any kind. But there would still be people in Mission Creek who'd think Dylan had murdered his own father.

"Bring me up to date and I'll consider your deal," Dylan said.

Hart nodded. "Two things. One: Erica Clawson thinks she remembers seeing a man getting in a car parked in the front parking lot when she first went outside on her break, before she saw your father's body in the pond. Two: The murder weapon has disappeared from the crime lab."

"Interesting." Dylan absorbed the information. "Even if the gun is missing, does it really matter? Y'all identified it as the murder weapon and the forensic guys didn't lift any prints off the gun, right? So why would anybody bother stealing it? And if Erica Clawson can't identify the person she thinks she saw, then what good does that do us?"

"Erica might remember more," Hart said. "She seemed awfully nervous when we questioned her."

"The girl did find a dead body," Maddie reminded him. "That's enough to make anybody nervous."

Hart shrugged. "The missing weapon is what concerns us. We hadn't made public the fact that there were no fingerprints found on the gun, so if it was stolen, whoever took it might have known something only a few people knew, only we insiders knew—Chief Terry had requested the gun be tested more thoroughly, for the lab to look for a palm print. Finding a palm print is always a long shot, but more than one criminal has been caught that way."

"Are you saying that y'all believe somebody inside the police department took the gun?" Maddie asked.

Hart grunted. "Either the police department or the sheriff's department. Looks like when we cleaned house, one rat might have eluded our trap. Either that or some new recruit has been bought off."

"Any ideas on who?" Dylan asked.

"Not a clue," Hart said. "But if there's still one rotten apple in the barrel, I'll find him."

"What about the palm print?" Dylan asked. "You said it was a long shot. Did—"

"Yeah, the lab lifted a palm print, but that will help us only if we bring in a suspect and can compare prints."

Maddie nudged Dylan. "Why don't we tell Hart who we think might have been behind your father's murder?"

Dylan contemplated her suggestion. If Hart O'Brien could trust him, then he should be able to trust Hart. "We think it's possible that either Carmine Mercado or Frank Del Brio hired a hit man to kill my dad."

Hart's eyes widened. "A mob hit?"

"A personal vendetta," Dylan said. "Because my father defended the four men accused of killing Haley Mercado and got them acquitted."

"I'd say we've come to the same conclusion—that it's a possibility one or both of those men were involved. And if our killer is a hit man, he's a sloppy one. I'd say he's some two-bit sleazeball hood."

"A wannabe hit man?" Maddie asked.

"Yeah, something like that. The guy made too many mistakes to be a true professional. The scheme to kill the judge could have been a hasty decision, thus the use of a local wise guy." Hart glanced at Dylan. "But without evidence, the police can't go pointing fingers at anyone in particular."

"Well, I'm not hampered by your rules and regulations," Dylan said. "I can—"

"You can wind up getting your butt put in jail, if somebody doesn't shoot you first."

Dylan harrumphed.

"There are other possibilities," Hart said. "We need to explore those before going off in the wrong direction."

"And what would the right direction be?" Maddie asked.

"Judge Bridges was on the bench for quite a few years and he sentenced a lot of people to prison. Until we rule out every criminal who ever threatened the judge's life—"

"Do you have a list of those people?"

"We've got a list, but we haven't had time to check out everyone. Not yet."

"Is that the only other possibility?" Dylan asked.

Hart shook his head. "A couple of months ago we had a baby left on the golf course, on the ninth tee.

Flynt and Josie Carson are foster parenting the child, a little girl named Lena.''

''What does this have to do with my father?''

''Maybe nothing,'' Hart said. ''But we've found out that Judge Bridges showed quite an interest in the child's welfare.''

''So?'' Dylan stared quizzically at Hart.

''It may be only a coincidence, but three of the four men who found baby Lena were defendants in the Haley Mercado murder case. And the fourth defendant was supposed to have been playing with them that morning, but a last-minute substitute took his place when he had to go out of town.''

''You're stretching a little there, aren't you, Detective?'' Dylan said.

''It's my job to consider every possibility. That way we make sure we're going after the right person.''

The moment they arrived at the Bridges house, Maddie spoke to the caterers she had hired. Dylan had given her free rein in organizing the post-funeral reception. She had not only arranged for the caterers, the fresh flowers and the string quartet, but she had made several phone calls to various friends letting them know how disappointed she'd be if they didn't stop by this evening. She'd be damned if she'd let anybody snub Dylan, regardless of their personal feelings or their suspicions about him. She had enough clout so that just the threat of her displeasure would assemble a nice crowd at the Bridges home.

She'd also used a threat to keep her mother away—and to silence Nadine's incessant warnings about Dylan. She'd told her mother plainly that she could and would discontinue paying for the upkeep of the huge mansion in which she resided so comfortably. Her mother would sulk for days and probably take to her bed with a sick headache, but at least she'd give Maddie a breather.

Everyone who was anyone in Mission Creek put in an appearance, some staying for ten minutes, others for a couple of hours. Strange how the death of a friend or close acquaintance brought people together.

Even though she'd been dazed by grief and thankfully numb after her father's funeral, she remembered bits and pieces of that evening. Everyone who'd known Jock Delarue had had a story to tell, and listening to various people reminiscing about her father had been comforting. She hoped that hearing about his father's life, told in vivid terms by his oldest and dearest friends, helped Dylan deal with the judge's death. Hadn't some wise person once said that you were never truly gone as long as there was one person alive who remembered you?

As the evening wore on, Maddie could sense exhaustion claiming Dylan. His broad shoulders slumped, his eyelids drooped occasionally, and she noticed he kept looking at his watch. She suspected that he hadn't slept more than a few hours each night since the judge's murder. And today, Dylan had gone through a lengthy funeral, then buried his father and spent the past three hours being a host. It was time for her to graciously rid the house of the stragglers, who were still drinking and reminiscing.

Fifteen minutes later Maddie waved goodbye to the string quartet as she ushered them out the back door. Only the catering staff remained to clean up.

Turning to Racine Borden, the caterer, Maddie said, "Thank you. Everything was lovely. Just perfect." Then she added, "I'd like a fresh pot of decaf coffee brought to the study, please. And when y'all finish up, just lock the back door on your way out."

"Yes, Ms. Delarue. And thank you for using Borden Catering."

As she entered the living room, Maddie found Dylan removing his jacket. "The caterers are finishing up and should be out of here soon. Until then, why don't we go sit down in the study? I've asked Ms. Borden to bring us some decaf coffee."

Dylan whipped off his tie and undid the top two buttons on his shirt. "That sounds like a good idea. I'm dead on my feet."

Maddie slipped her arm through his and walked him down the hall and into the study. "This has been a long day. You look beat." She led him to an old, overstuffed sofa. "Sit and relax."

He did as she requested and sat, leaned his head

against the back of the sofa and closed his eyes. "God, I'm tired."

"You haven't been sleeping, have you?" Maddie sat beside him.

He lifted his eyelids and gave her a sidelong glance. "I can't begin to tell you how many times since Dad's murder that I've dreamed about his body floating in the pond. And like most dreams, they've been surreal and all mixed up. I keep hearing laughter. And seeing fingers pointing. And twice—" he swallowed hard "—twice I've dreamed that the townsfolk lynched me. Strung me up at the courthouse."

"Oh, Dylan." Scooting closer, she grabbed his hand. "No rational person would believe you killed your father."

He squeezed her hand, then let go and rubbed his forehead. Apparently overcome with frustration, he slammed his fist down on his thigh. "I didn't kill my dad, but maybe I could have done something to have prevented his murder."

"What do you think you could have done?" She recognized the emotion that rode him so hard—guilt. After her father died, she'd felt guilty, but had eventually come to realize that it was a common reaction among family and close friends when a person died. In the weeks and months after Jock Delarue's death, she had thought of all the things she wished she'd said and done while he was alive. No doubt Dylan was now experiencing that same sense of regret.

"If I hadn't let so many years go by before I came home, then I'd have been here for him when he needed me. If we'd had a long-standing father-and-son relationship, I'd have known if somebody was threatening him. He would have told me if he was in trouble."

"It's only natural to wish you could have done something that would have changed things."

"Is it?" He turned to Maddie, his gaze locking with hers. "You have no idea how guilty I feel. I keep thinking that it's all my fault, that if I'd been a better son..." Dylan's voice cracked. He jerked around, putting his back to her.

Oh, God, help him, Maddie prayed. He's hurting in the worst way possible. When she laid her hand on his back, he tensed.

Dylan cleared his throat. "Why don't you go on home? You've got to be exhausted, too."

"I don't want to leave you alone."

He snorted. "Why? Do you think I'll fall apart without you?"

"No, of course not. It's just that—"

He whirled around, tension and anger etched on his features. "Look, Red, I've had about as much as I can stand of your sympathy. Stop hovering over me. You're driving me nuts."

Maddie felt as if he'd slapped her. She stared at him, her gaze questioning his unkind comments.

Racine Borden knocked, then opened the study door

and brought in a silver coffee service and placed the tray on the desk by the windows. ''Here's the coffee you requested. We're almost finished and will be leaving shortly.''

''Thank you,'' Maddie said, then rose from the sofa, walked over to the desk and poured herself a cup of coffee.

The minute the caterer left the room, Maddie asked, ''Would you likc some?''

''No. I don't want any coffee. I want to be left alone.''

She glanced down at the china cup she held in her hand. ''Do you mind if I drink this before I leave?''

''Hell, Maddie, just go, will you? Fix yourself some damn coffee at home.''

What was wrong with him? she asked herself. Why all of a sudden had he turned on her, venting his frustration and rage directly at her? Think about it, Maddie. He almost broke down and cried in front of you just a few minutes ago. He's let you get too close, let you see his vulnerability, something most men hate with a passion. He wants to warn you off before he loses control. The last thing on earth a man like Dylan Bridges would want was for someone to see him in a moment of weakness.

''I'll go.'' She placed the cup and saucer on the silver tray. ''I realize you'll be just fine without me.'' Turn the tables on him, she told herself. Let him know that you're the one in need right now. Let him show you his strength. "But I'm not so sure how well I'll do without you."

She walked to the door, then paused and glanced over her shoulder. "I guess wanting to stay here with you was selfish on my part. I dread going home to my big, empty condo. I'm not quite as strong as you are. I hate being alone when I'm so sad and unhappy and—"

"Drink your coffee before you go," he said.

"No. I...no, thanks. I'll be all right. I'm used to being alone. It's just that for tonight, I'd hoped—"

While Maddie watched in astonishment, Dylan rose from the sofa and lunged across the room. She held her breath as he grabbed her, then she sighed when he pulled her into his arms. She leaned against him as his embrace surrounded her and he pressed his cheek against hers.

"I'm sorry, honey. I wasn't thinking about anybody except myself."

She slipped her arms around his waist and rested her head on his chest. He stroked her back soothingly. Bless him, he was comforting her. He was the one in charge now, the strong, commanding male.

"Come on back." He led her to the sofa, seated her and then went to the desk and picked up her cup and saucer. "Here you go, Red. Drink your coffee." After handing her coffee to her, he returned to the desk and prepared himself a cup. "We had a nice crowd here tonight, didn't we? I was surprised that so many people showed up. I figured they'd stay away in droves. Maybe everybody in town doesn't think I killed my father."

"No one thinks that," she said, knowing her statement was a little white lie. But what did it matter as long as it made Dylan feel better?

They sat together on the sofa for hours and drank the decaf coffee and talked, both making sure the conversation never became too personal and didn't delve too deeply into Dylan's emotions. Sometime before midnight, they both fell asleep sitting together in the study. At two, Maddie woke and realized she was cuddled up against Dylan, her head on his shoulder. She stood, stretched and gazed down at him. He stirred, but didn't wake, then he slumped over so that his head touched the arm rest. Maddie lifted his long legs and placed them on the sofa. When she removed his shoes, he murmured something unintelligible. She lifted a large knit afghan from the back of the sofa and draped it over Dylan.

"Thanks for needing me," she whispered as she leaned down to kiss his cheek. "And thanks for not seeing through my little ploy."

Leaving him sleeping soundly, Maddie let herself out and headed home in the wee hours of the warm August morning.

Nine

In her home office, Maddie gathered her files together and placed them in her briefcase. The annual Labor Day barbeque at the country club was only a couple of weeks away and there was still a great deal to do. Thankfully, Alicia had turned out to be a godsend. The young woman was, without a doubt, the best assistant Maddie had ever had. And this past week having a topnotch assistant had been vital, freeing Maddie several afternoons to go off with Dylan in their continuing efforts to unearth information that might lead them to Carl Bridges' murderer.

So far, they'd come up with nothing that put them any closer to solving the crime. True to his word, Hart had kept them posted on the police investigation, which seemed to be going nowhere. And with each passing day, Dylan became more disheartened. But the more hopeless things seemed, the more determined he became not to stop searching, despite Hart's cautions to let the police handle the matter.

As she walked through the living room, Maddie deposited her briefcase and purse on the mahogany table in the foyer, then headed straight toward the delicious aroma coming from the kitchen. Anticipating Thelma's homemade cinnamon rolls, Maddie swung open the door and followed the spicy scent. Thelma emptied a pan of freshly baked rolls onto a plate in the center of the oval, oak table.

“Good morning.” Maddie sniffed, sighed and pulled out a chair. “To what do I owe the honor of being served cinnamon rolls this morning?”

Thelma dumped the hot pan in the sink, then poured a cup of gourmet coffee into a ceramic mug and placed it on the paisley placemat in front of Maddie. “You said that as if I never prepare fresh-baked rolls for you.”

“You don't.” Before Thelma could defend herself, Maddie added, “And it's because I've asked you not to. Your pies and cakes are delicious, too, but so tempting.” Maddie patted her round hips. “Every extra bite of sugar goes right here. It's the curse of all short, curvy women.”

“Humph.” Thelma surveyed Maddie's figure. “You're built like a goddess and you know it.”

Maddie grinned. Thelma was always good for her cgo, just likc a mothcr should bc. Evcryonc clsc's mother except her own. Nadine tended to notice whenever Maddie gained a pound and never missed an opportunity to tell her.

“How's Dylan?” Thelma asked.

“He's fine. Why do you ask?”

''Just curious. I've kind of been expecting to see him here for breakfast one morning.''

Maddie's mouth dropped open. ''Ah, I see. You actually baked these cinnamon rolls for Dylan.''

Thelma shrugged. ''Well, you two have been more or less attached at the hip since he came back to town, and you've been gallivanting all over the place with him since the judge's funeral. I figured that sooner or later he'd spend the night here.''

''I don't usually hop into bed with a man after seeing him for only two weeks.'' Maddie lifted her mug and sipped the coffee, then reached over and pinched off a bite from one of the hot rolls.

''You don't usually hop into bed with a man after seeing him for two years,'' Thelma countered. ''But Dylan Bridges is different. He's not like all the other men who've paraded in and out of your life.''

''Yes, he is different. Dylan and I are friends.''

''Friends and lovers.''

Maddie huffed. ''We are not lovers.''

''Not yet, but it's only a matter of time. You're falling in love with that man and there's no need for you to deny it.''

''I'm not. I—I like Dylan a lot, but I don't intend to let myself fall in love with him. He and I agree that we're both lousy at relationships. But we need each other right now. As friends.''

''Just be sure that when y'all finally get around to making love, that you use the proper protection.''

Thelma separated one of the rolls from the others, placed it on a small plate and set it in front of Maddie, then handed her a fork. ''You could wind up pregnant and unmarried. That's probably what happened to little baby Lena's mama.''

''My goodness, Thelma, I'm thirty-three, not sixteen. I do know how to prevent pregnancy and protect myself from disease.''

''Speaking of little Lena—''

''Ah-ha!'' Maddie pointed her fork at Thelma. ''You're dying to tell me some bit of juicy gossip you've collected from that grapevine of busybody housekeepers and maids that seems to have more news than the *Clarion.*''

''We have inquiring minds and we're all interested in our fellow man, which is our Christian duty.''

Maddie grinned, then sliced off a piece of gooey roll and lifted it to her mouth. Gossip was to Thelma what breathing was to other humans; without it, she'd die.

''Do you or do you not want to hear the news?''

Chewing and enjoying, Maddie nodded.

''Well, the private eye that the golf foursome who found Baby Lena hired—I think his name is Aston—found out from the blood tests that little Lena has something called thalassemia.''

''Mmm-hmm.'' Maddie ate another bite of cinnamon roll.

''In case you don't know, it's some funny type of

anemia that's common to people of Mediterranean descent. And that means either the child's mama or daddy is Mediterranean. Maybe Italian. What do you think about that?''

''I think it's very interesting.''

''If Lena belongs to one of those Mercados or that Del Brio man or some of that bunch, then she's better off staying with Flynt and Josie Carson for the rest of her life.'' Thelma poured herself a mug of coffee and sat across from Maddie. ''And if Dylan keeps sniffing around the wrong Italians, trying to find out if Carl Bridges' murder was mob related, then he could wind up in big trouble—or maybe dead like the judge.''

''How did you know that Dylan has been— Forget I asked. Of course you'd know. I'm surprised that the police haven't come to you for help, considering your network of domestic spies.''

Thelma laughed, a boisterous cackle that projected loudly through the condo. ''I was going to share some more news, but since you're being so snippy, I just might not tell you.''

Maddie gazed pleadingly across the table at Thelma. ''I wasn't being snippy. I was paying you a compliment.''

''A backhanded compliment if I ever heard one.''

''Ah, come on, Thelma, give. You don't want me to be the last to know the latest gossip, do you?''

''Well, I suppose not.'' Thelma sipped her coffee, eyed Maddie over the rim of the mug, then sighed dramatically and said, "Another of the prime daddy candidates has been eliminated by the DNA tests."

"Which one?"

"Dr. Michael O'Day," Thelma said. "But I hear they're doing more testing before they officially eliminate Tyler Murdoch. Personally, I don't think he's the daddy either."

"Are you by any chance taking odds on who the father is?"

"It's just speculation, but rumor has it that the other prime candidates are wondering if maybe Luke Callaghan is the proud papa. And you know that nobody's seen hide nor hair of Luke lately."

"Gee, Thelma, I'm glad that Dylan and I only have a murder mystery to solve and not a paternity puzzle to figure out."

"Could be there's a connection between the two." Thelma lifted her brows and widened her eyes in a what-do-you-think-of-that gesture.

"You're the second person who's suggested that the judge's death might somehow be linked to Baby Lena." Maddie leaned forward and looked directly at her housekeeper. "What could the connection possibly be?"

"That I don't know." Thelma finished off her coffee, scooted back her chair and stood. "Might not be any connection. But then again, who knows?"

Maddie opened her mouth to reply, but before she got out the first word, the phone rang.

Thelma hopped up and lifted the receiver from the wall base. "Ms. Delarue's residence." Pause. "Yeah, sure thing. She's here." Thelma held out the receiver. "It's Dylan."

Maddie jumped up out of the chair, licked the tips of her fingers, then grabbed the phone. When Thelma grinned at Maddie, she made a face at her housekeeper.

"Hello," Maddie said.

"Hi, Red. Any chance you can take off from work around lunchtime and give me a couple of hours?"

"Sure. I can manage a long lunch break today." Actually, she couldn't, not with all the work she'd pushed aside in the past week. But if Dylan needed her, wanted her, she was not going to let him down. Once again, she'd ask Alicia to take over. Maddie had made a mental note to give Alicia a bonus from her private account. "So, what's up?"

"I spoke to Dad's attorney, Dennis Barber, and set up a meeting today to go over the will."

"You want me to go with you," she said. "I can meet you there at—"

"No, let me pick you up, then afterward we can eat a late lunch together. How does that sound?"

"Sounds great." She knew that Dylan had been putting off Dennis Barber's request for them to move forward and have the judge's will probated. He'd told her that he wasn't quite ready to face that task. She understood. Even with billions of dollars in Jock Delarue's estate, she'd found it difficult to listen to her father's last will and testament. Reading the will had made her father's death seem more final.

"Pick you up at one," Dylan said. "And Maddie...thanks."

The minute Maddie returned the receiver to the wall base, Thelma grinned at her. "Having a long, private lunch with Dylan today, are we?"

"Don't press your luck with me," Maddie joked. "You could be replaced, you know."

Thelma laughed. "Not much chance of that. I'm irreplaceable and we both know it."

Maddie rolled her eyes heavenward. "For your information, I'm going with Dylan to Dennis Barber's office to discuss Judge Bridges' will."

"That could be good and bad for Dylan."

"What do you mean? How could it be bad for him?"

"I'd say the judge left Dylan everything and that would be good from one standpoint. But with Dylan being the only beneficiary, that means he'd have a motive for murder."

"Don't be ridiculous. Who'd believe Dylan would kill his father for money? Dylan has millions and I doubt Judge Bridges did."

"Dylan's worth millions, huh?" Thelma grinned. "I'd heard he was filthy rich, but now I know for sure."

"Very clever. You wormed that information out of me as easy as that." Maddie snapped her fingers.

"I didn't worm anything out of you, missy. Is it my fault that in defending Dylan you just happened to mention how rich he is?"

"The point I was making is that even if Carl Bridges left Dylan everything, the police can't possibly see that as a motive."

"I agree. But mark my word, rumors will fly once the judge's will is probated." When Maddie frowned, Thelma said, "There's nothing you can do about it, so stop worrying. People are going to talk. Best thing Dylan can do is ignore them."

"I hope he doesn't hear any more whispered innuendoes. He's having a difficult enough time dealing with his father's murder without having to endure people's ridiculous speculations."

"So, you aren't falling in love with Dylan Bridges, huh? Just listen to yourself, Maddie. You're fighting mad and ready to whip the world to protect that man. I'd say, whether you like it or not, you're a goner."

After Dennis Barber read Carl Bridges' will, Dylan sat quietly in the lawyer's office, his solemn gaze riveted to the floor. Dennis cleared his throat. Dylan ignored him. Maddie wanted to tell Dennis not to push Dylan, to give him time to absorb the news that his father had indeed left his entire estate to him. The judge's net worth had been a little more than Maddie imagined it would be, but well within the norm for a successful circuit judge who had made some wise investments.

"Do you have any questions?" Dennis asked.

Dylan glanced at the lawyer and shook his head.

"Well, then—" Dennis lifted a set of keys from his desk drawer and held them out to Dylan "—here's the keys to your father's safety deposit box at the bank. I've already notified them over at First Federal that I'm turning over the contents of Carl's box to you, as per instructions in his will."

Dylan rose to his feet, reached out and accepted the keys. "You were Dad's co-signer on the box, right?"

"That's right."

"Have you taken a look inside the box since Dad's death?"

"I've never looked inside the judge's safety deposit box," Dennis replied. "I was co-signer for one reason only—so that I could turn the contents over to you."

"Haven't the police asked about the contents?" Dylan asked.

"They did and I told them that to my knowledge, other than CDs and other such documents, the only thing in the box was another copy of Carl's will and…some personal mementos that had belonged to your mother. Her wedding band and engagement ring and some photographs of her."

Maddie noted the tension in Dylan. The clenched jaw. The tight lips. The unfocused gaze. It was all she could do to keep herself from putting her arm around him.

"Detective O'Brien did request that when you opened the safety deposit box, if you found anything—"

"Undoubtedly the police don't think there'll be anything of significance inside," Dylan said. "Otherwise, they'd have gotten a court order to take a look at the contents."

"I agree." Dennis held out his hand to Dylan. "I'll give you a call soon. And in the meantime, if there's anything I can do, don't hesitate to let me know."

Dylan shook the lawyer's hand. "Thanks." He glanced at Maddie, then nodded toward the door.

Placing his hand at her elbow, he guided her from the office, down the corridor and to the elevator. With several other occupants already inside, neither Dylan nor Maddie spoke on the elevator's descent to the lobby. But once they were outside and in Dylan's Porsche, Maddie thought surely he would say something. He didn't. Instead he sat there behind the wheel, his eyes glazed as he stared off into nothingness.

Unable to endure his silence a moment longer, Maddie spoke his name. "Dylan?"

"Yeah, I'm okay, honey. Just putting off doing what I need to do."

He glanced at her then and she thought her heart would break. Maybe no one else could have seen past that weak smile and the false bravado of the hard-as-nails, unemotional male, but Maddie could. Dylan dreaded going through the judge's safety deposit box and having to look at the personal items Dennis Barber had mentioned. Pictures of Leda Bridges, the mother he'd lost at twelve. And the engagement ring and wedding band his father had placed on his beloved's finger.

"I'll be there with you," she told him. "If you'd like, I can go through the box for you and—"

Instantly he reached over and caressed her face, his fingers lingering on her cheek. "You're a born caretaker, aren't you, sweet Maddie? And you seem to know me so well."

"Like I've said before, I believe you and I are two of a kind. It's not that difficult to figure out what you're feeling when it's often exactly what I'd be feeling, if I were you."

"I can handle going through the box," he told her. "But I won't mind having company while I'm doing it."

Fifteen minutes later, they stood side-by-side at the bank, the contents of the judge's safety deposit box emptied onto a table in a private nook within the large vault.

"Pretty much what Dennis said would be here." Dylan sorted through the various items, mostly papers and documents, everything from over a hundred thousand dollars in CDs to copies of Carl and Leda's marriage certificate, Carl's, Leda's and Dylan's birth certificates, and a small box of photographs.

Dylan picked up a velvet pouch, opened it and dumped the contents into the palm of his hand. Maddie watched him as he gazed down at the plain gold band and the one-carat solitaire diamond.

"Mama told me once that she scolded Dad for spending so much money on her engagement ring," Dylan said. "Having been raised poor, Mama thought a one-carat diamond was very extravagant." He eased the engagement ring onto the tip of his index finger, then studied it closely. "She told me that when I grew up and found the girl I wanted to marry, she intended to give me this ring for my bride."

"Oh, Dylan, what a dear, sweet sentiment."

He dropped both rings into the velvet pouch and placed them back in the metal box, then dumped the photographs from the box and spread them out on top of the other papers. Maddie looked at the pictures, mainly black-and-white snapshots of his parents. But in the middle of the old photos, several studio-quality pictures of a baby caught Maddie's attention.

"May I take a closer look at these?" She pointed to the baby pictures.

"Sure, go ahead. I noticed them," Dylan said, "but I don't recognize that child."

Maddie studied the photos of a baby girl with big blue eyes and dark curly hair. "This child resembles Lena. She's the little girl who was abandoned on the country club golf course a few months ago, the child that Josie and Flynt Carson are taking care of.''

''Are you sure?'' Dylan grabbed the photos. ''Why would my father have pictures of the abandoned baby?''

''Good question.''

''Hart said that my dad showed an interest in Baby Lena, right? And we know that three of the four men Dad defended in the Haley Mercado murder case were together playing golf when they found the child. Now we discover photos of that child in my father's safety deposit box. Could there really be a connection between this child and my father's murder?''

''Maybe. But it could be only a coincidence. And concentrating on the baby might lead us off in the wrong direction.''

Slumping his shoulders, Dylan sighed. ''I'm going to leave everything here at the bank for now.'' He gathered up the items and arranged them in the safety deposit box, but slipped the photos of the baby girl into his pocket.

A few minutes later when they left the bank, Dylan pulled out the photos and looked at them again. He frowned.

''What's wrong?'' Maddie asked.

''Nothing. I just had a crazy thought. But looking at this child, I see no resemblance to my father.'' He held up one of the photos. ''Do you see any?''

"Oh, Dylan, you can't think that little Lena is your father's child."

"No, not really. I told you it was a crazy thought."

"You're grasping at straws." Maddie slipped her arm through his. "Come on. Let's go to the club and have a late lunch in the café."

"Yeah...okay."

"What's wrong now?"

"Nothing really, just thinking about one other source of possible information."

"And that source would be?" she asked.

"My dad has a safe at home. One of those old wall safes behind a picture in his den."

"Why haven't you already checked the contents?"

"Because I don't have the combination," Dylan told her. "Besides, I think the only thing he kept in there was some cash and an old Smith & Wesson revolver that belonged to his uncle."

"Maybe a locksmith could get the safe open for you."

"Maybe. I'll look into it soon." He guided her to his Porsche, then unlocked and opened the door for her. "Right now, I'd rather have lunch with the prettiest girl in Mission Creek."

Smiling, Maddie slipped into the passenger seat. "Are we going to pick her up on the way to the club or is she meeting us there?"

Dylan leaned down and into the Porsche, bringing his face close to Maddie's. "Neither. She's already right here, close enough for me to kiss.'' He brushed his lips over hers.

Maddie's stomach flipflopped. If Dylan's compliments weren't sincere, she didn't want to ever learn the truth. Don't doubt him, an inner voice advised. If she couldn't trust Dylan, she'd never be able to trust anyone.

With the humid August breeze doing little more than fanning the heat around them, Maddie and Dylan headed for the club. As they sped along Gulf Road, a late-model dark sedan with tinted windows came up right behind them.

''Why doesn't he just come on and go around me instead of riding my bumper that way?'' Dylan glared into the rearview mirror.

''That car has been behind us since we left the bank,'' Maddie said.

''I didn't notice it until a few minutes ago.'' Dylan waved his arm, motioning for the closely following vehicle to pass. ''There's nothing coming from the other direction. I don't know why he doesn't—''

The sedan sped out from behind the Porsche and came up alongside it in the opposite lane, but made no attempt to pass.

''What the hell is he doing?'' Dylan grumbled.

Suddenly the sedan skidded straight over, ramming into the side of the Porsche. Dylan cursed loudly.

Maddie grabbed the edge of her seat. Had the driver

of the other car lost control? Oh, God, were they going to crash?

Dylan pressed his foot down on the accelerator, sped forward and momentarily left the sedan behind. But within moments the other vehicle caught up with them and repeated the first staggering blow with a second, followed by a quick, hard third. Dylan struggled to maintain control of his car, but when the maniacal driver lunged the sedan into the Porsche a fourth time, the Porsche skidded off the road and crashed into a steep ditch.

The car surged to a violent stop, and only their secure seat belts saved Maddie and Dylan from being tossed into the windshield. By the time Dylan undid his safety belt and turned to Maddie, the dark sedan had sailed off down the road and quickly disappeared.

"Are you all right, honey?" Dylan unsnapped Maddie's seat belt and ran his hands over her from neck to waist.

"I—I'm okay. I think. God, Dylan, what just happened?"

He cupped her face with his hands. "Tell me again that you're okay."

His hands were shaking and his voice quivered with fear. He was so concerned about her welfare that he was trembling. "I'm all right," she told him.

He nodded, then released her. "That idiot could have killed us."

"It wasn't an accident, was it?"

"No. Whoever was driving that car had every intention of running us off the road."

"But why would—"

Dylan's cell phone rang. He cursed under his breath, then removed the phone from his belt clip and flipped it open.

"Bridges here," he said.

"I understand you just had an accident, Mr. Bridges."

Because of her close proximity to Dylan, Maddie could hear the voice. She leaned closer and when Dylan tried to move the phone to his other ear, she grabbed his hand, then leaned closer until her ear was pressed against the other side of the phone.

"Who is this?" Dylan asked.

"Just a man with some good advice for you."

"And what would that be?"

"If you keep digging for information in the wrong places, keep sticking your nose in the family's business, then you and your girlfriend are going to get hurt. Hurt bad. Today was just a sample of what could happen to you. Next time it'll be worse."

Ten

With the big country club barbeque coming up this weekend, Maddie decided to work late tonight and tie up all the loose ends. And if she were completely honest with herself, she'd admit that she simply did not want to go home to her big, empty condo. These past couple of weeks had been the longest, most miserable of her life. And all because of Dylan Bridges. Stubborn mule! After their close brush with disaster and the warning phone call, Dylan had told her that her days playing amateur sleuth were over.

"I won't be responsible for your getting hurt," he'd told her. "From now on, I'll be flying solo, honey. I do not want you involved."

"But I am involved."

"Not any longer."

He'd been adamant about ending not only their Nick and Nora Charles act, but their personal relationship, too. No amount of arguing or pleading had swayed him one iota. For the first week she had tried showing up at his house every day, only to be sent away again and again. A couple of times, she had followed him, but he'd managed to get away from her.

Her phone messages were not returned, and the few times he'd actually answered his phone, he'd told her in no uncertain terms to leave him the hell alone.

Maddie reminded herself that Dylan thought he was protecting her by staying away from her. But she didn't feel protected. She felt lonely, abandoned and in desperate need of one of Dylan's marvelous smiles. She had become quickly addicted to his unassuming charm and was now having severe withdrawal symptoms.

Admit the truth, she told herself. Thelma was right. You were beginning to fall in love with Dylan. Okay, so she was halfway in love with the man. If he didn't return her feelings, she simply shouldn't allow herself to care so much. But how did she stop herself from caring? How could she give up the hope that Dylan loved her, too? But if he continued keeping her at arm's length, what chance would Dylan have to discover that he loved her?

If only the police would find Carl Bridges' murderer. But it seemed that they were no closer now to making an arrest than they'd been the night the judge had been killed. And Hart had told her that despite the warning from "the family," Dylan hadn't stopped digging into matters best handled by the law. She should be helping him. What if he got into trouble? Dammit, why didn't the man realize how much he needed her?

Maddie yawned. She hadn't slept well lately and

had kept herself so busy that she was exhausted. Maybe it was time to call it a night and head home. She could think about Dylan at home just as easily as she could here at the club. It really didn't matter where she was or what she was doing, thoughts of Dylan crept into her mind.

Suddenly Maddie heard an odd noise, as if something had fallen in the outer office. But at ten-thirty there was no one here tonight, except her. Even the club and the restaurants were all closed by now.

Footsteps. Was that what she heard? Maddie listened. Silence. Was her imagination working overtime?

This late at night, there would be only two security guards at the club. One was stationed outside and the second one kept watch at a closed-circuit television behind the registration desk in the lobby. Just call downstairs and ask the guard to come up and check things out, she told herself. What does it matter if he doesn't find anything? Better safe than sorry.

Maddie lifted the telephone receiver to her ear as she poised her index finger over the buttons. She hit the one that would ring the front desk. Nothing. That was odd. She tried again. Still nothing. She punched the nine for an outside line. No dial tone. Don't panic, she cautioned herself. Just walk across the room and lock the door, then use your cell phone to call for help. Do it. Do it now!

Maddie shoved back her chair, stood and then ran

toward the door. Her heart raced, the beat thundering in her ears. She slammed the door closed, then grabbed the handle with the intention of locking the door. A powerful force shoved the door open and a large, dark hand reached out and grabbed her. Before she caught more than a quick glimpse of the side of his swarthy face covered by a sheer stocking, he twisted her around so that her back was up against his chest. As she opened her mouth to scream, he gagged her with his open palm.

His hot breath fanned her neck as his lips grazed her ear. ''Tell Dylan Bridges to be on the next plane to Dallas. And if he isn't, then I'll pay you another visit and I won't be so nice next time. I'll slit your throat. Tell him that, too.''

Dylan drove ninety to nothing in his haste to get to the country club. The deep, menacing voice over the phone had told him that he should go see his girlfriend, that she had a message for him. The call had come in five minutes ago while Dylan was driving home from the Mission Creek Café, where he'd eaten a late supper.

''What have you done to Maddie?'' Dylan had demanded.

''Other than give her an important message for you?'' The guy had laughed. ''Why don't you run over to the country club and find out for yourself what's been done to her?''

When Dylan couldn't reach Maddie at her office number, fear ate away at his insides like an insidious acid, destroying slowly but surely. If Maddie was hurt…God help the bastard who had harmed her.

As he parked his rental car under the canopied entrance to the club, Dylan begged God not to let any harm come to Maddie. Sweet, beautiful Maddie, who was so innocent in all this dirty, rotten mess. Once again, because of her association with him, she was in trouble. Big trouble this time. He'd tried to put some distance between them in order to keep her safe, but apparently the bad guys realized just how much Maddie Delarue meant to him.

Dylan rushed to the front door. Locked! He beat on the glass until the security guard appeared.

"Let me in," he screamed. "Maddie— Ms. Delarue is in trouble. Someone's in her office to harm her. Right now. Dammit, man, let me in."

Curt Dodd unlocked the door. Dylan rushed in right past the guard, who called out to him, "Hey, hold up there."

"I phoned the police on my way here," Dylan said. "Keep a lookout for them while I go up and check on Maddie."

"But you don't have a weapon," Curt called out, but Dylan was already on the waiting elevator.

Hurry. Go faster. Damn! Why hadn't he taken the stairs? The elevator doors swung open. Dylan ran down the corridor and straight to Maddie's office suite. The door stood open, revealing a darkened interior. Only a dim light came from beyond the outer office, from somewhere inside Maddie's private domain. Dylan paused and listened. He heard mumbling that sounded like a man's voice speaking soft and low.

Adrenaline pumped through Dylan's system at supersonic speed. In that instant all pretense of the civilized male disappeared from his chemical makeup. He was primitive man, primed and ready to defend his mate—to the death if necessary. He walked quietly into Alicia's office and snaked softly around the wall until he reached the wide open door to Maddie's office. Inside a brass banker's lamp burned softly on the ornate mahogany desk, and gave off a dim glow that cast shadows on the walls.

A man whose stocking-masked face was partially blocked by Maddie's head held her in front of him, one arm draped across her throat while his other arm moved up and down across her body, his hands caressing her roughly. Bright red rage boiled inside Dylan. He'd kill the son of a bitch.

"Maybe I ought to find out for myself just what Dylan Bridges likes about you, other than the obvious."

Dylan didn't see any sign of a weapon on the guy, but weapon or no weapon, it didn't matter to him. As long as Maddie was in no danger of being shot or stabbed, he'd take his chances. Like a raging bull, Dylan charged into the office. Before her assailant realized what was happening, he grabbed the man, which instantly freed Maddie from his hold. She reeled to one side, then being temporarily unbalanced, fell to the floor. The guy swung at Dylan, who sidestepped the first punch; then Dylan landed a hard blow to the man's belly. The attacker groaned loudly as he doubled over. When Dylan moved in for the kill, something hit him over the head and knocked him to his knees. For a split second everything went black, then his vision returned. Fuzzy. Unfocused. Looking back over his shoulder, he tried to stand and saw the blurred images of two men rushing through the door. Two? Had there been two, or was he seeing double?

Maddie shoved herself onto her knees then lifted herself up and onto her feet. "Dylan!"

He staggered as he tried to stand. "Maddie? Maddie, honey, are you all right?"

"Yes, thanks to you." She rushed to him, put her left arm around his waist and lifted her right hand to the top of his head. "He hit you with the butt of his gun."

"He had a gun?"

"Yes. The other man had a gun."

"Then there were two of them?"

"Yes, the one you were fighting with and the one who hit you over the head."

"They didn't hurt you, did they?" Dylan grabbed her by the shoulders and stared into her eyes. "When

I saw the way he was touching you… God, Maddie, I'm sorry. This was all my fault. They came after you as a warning to me."

"How did you—? How could you have known about them?"

"I got a phone call." He wrapped his arms around her and pulled her close. "Undoubtedly whoever hired those goons to come here called me a little prematurely. He probably didn't pay the guy to feel you up." Dylan rubbed his cheek against hers. "He thought they'd be gone by the time I got here."

"I have never been so scared in my life," she admitted.

"Yeah, honey, me, too. If anything had happened to you… God, Maddie, what have I gotten you into?"

Someone cleared their throat. Someone standing in the doorway. Maddie tensed, then glanced over Dylan's shoulder and sighed with relief when she saw Hart O'Brien.

"That's what I'd like to know," Hart said. "What have you gotten her into with your nosing around in stuff that's police business?"

Dylan didn't release his tenacious hold on Maddie; he simply eased her around as he turned to face Hart. "Did you catch them?"

"Nope. But a couple of black-and-whites are in pursuit right now."

"When you catch them, I want to—"

Maddie placed two fingers over Dylan's mouth.

"You're not going to do anything until we take you to the hospital and let a doctor examine you."

"What happened to you?" Hart asked.

"Nothing," Dylan replied.

"One of the guys hit Dylan over the head with the butt of his gun."

Hart lifted his eyebrows in a contemplating gesture. "If the guy had a gun, why didn't he just shoot you?"

"I think his orders were to scare Maddie," Dylan said. "Not kill anyone."

"One of you want to tell me exactly what happened?" Hart asked. "I was told that Dylan Bridges called in and said that someone was going to attack Maddie Delarue in her office at the country club."

"Do you mind if we fill you in on the details after I take Dylan to the hospital?" Maddie shoved against Dylan's chest so that he loosened his death grip on her.

"I don't need to go to the hospital," Dylan assured her.

She reached up, felt the bump on his head and tsk-tsked. "You've got a lump the size of a golf ball. I'm taking you to Mission Creek Memorial." She glanced at Hart. "Follow us, will you?"

"Maddie, I'm all right." Dylan balked when she tried to lead him toward the door.

"You might as well go peacefully," Hart said. "If she's anything like Joan—and I figure she is—she's not going to take no for an answer."

Dylan looked at Maddie. ''Will it make you feel better if I—''

''Yes!''

Three and a half hours later, Maddie and Dylan opened the front door of the Bridges home at 1010 Royal Avenue. Hart had sent a black-and-white to follow them and stay posted outside all night. He'd offered a policeman to escort Maddie home, but she'd told him that she'd be staying the night at Dylan's because he'd been diagnosed with a mild concussion and couldn't be left alone.

''I'm all right, dammit,'' Dylan said as he jerked away from Maddie. ''Stop treating me as if I'm dying.''

''Sorry.'' She eased away from him. Why hadn't she learned by now that Dylan didn't like to be smothered with attention? Every time she got too close to that little-boy vulnerability that existed in him, as it did in all men, he pulled away from her. A defense mechanism inherent in all macho guys? she wondered.

''No, honey, I'm the one who's sorry,'' he reached out and ruffled her hair. His hand lingered; his fingers spread apart, burrowed through her hair and gripped the back of her head. He stared directly into her eyes. ''You don't know how sorry I am that I ever got you involved in my problems.''

''I volunteered,'' she told him. ''You didn't force me. Heck, you didn't even ask.''

"Yeah, but look where that big heart of yours has gotten you. Right in the middle of a dangerous situation." Keeping his hold on the back of her head, he pulled her toward him. "If anything had happened to you tonight—"

She pressed her fingertips over his lips. "I'm all right. The only thing that happened was that those men frightened me. You're the one who got hurt."

"What hurt me the most was knowing that I put you in that situation. Can you ever forgive me?"

He looked at her with such hunger in his eyes that the intensity of his gaze sent shivers of pure awareness through her body. "There's nothing to forgive."

"Maddie...God, I've missed you, honey."

He kissed her. Hard, passionate and possessive.

Maddie's bones seemed to dissolve into warm liquid as the heat between her thighs grew hotter and hotter. Dylan was the only man who'd ever made her feel this way. Consumed by a primitive desire, she longed for him to take her. Here and now. Without any preamble. Just raw, savage mating.

He kissed her. And kissed her. And kissed her again. His mouth pressed, then withdrew. Then pressed again. He covered her face and throat with kisses before returning to her mouth. His tongue circled and tasted. His teeth nipped and pulled gently. And when she trembled, he tightened his hold on her head, held her forcefully in place and kissed her with a thoroughness that took her breath away.

Hunger exploded inside her, becoming a ravaging beast guided solely by the need for appeasement. She jerked his shirt open, popping buttons in her urgency. Her hands were everywhere on his body—stroking his chest, lightly dusted with pale brown hair; caressing his neck; flicking his tiny nipples; struggling to unbuckle his belt. Dylan responded by lifting her cotton sweater over her rib cage, which prompted her to lift her arms so that he could remove the garment. While she returned to her efforts to undo his belt, he unhooked her bra. They tore at each other's clothes, tossing a sock here, a shoe there. His briefs landed on the coffee table; her panties flew across the room and sailed beneath the sofa.

Naked, fully aroused and disregarding logical thought, they kissed, they fondled, they panted breathlessly. Dylan lifted Maddie off her feet, hoisting her up so that she could wrap her legs around his hips. He maneuvered her this way and that until he aligned her perfectly to take the full thrust of his sex as he shoved up and into her. Maddie cried out with pure, earth-shattering pleasure, the feel of him inside her glorious beyond words.

Gripping her hips, he moved her up and down. His groans echoed in her ears, the hungry grunts of an aroused male. While Maddie held on to him, her breasts rubbing against him, from neck to mid-chest, he pumped into her. Suddenly she felt the wall at her back and realized that Dylan had eased them several feet across the living room. Braced by the wall, Maddie grabbed his shoulders and flung her head back. Dylan kissed her neck, then licked a moist line across the top of her breasts. Her nipples tightened to diamond-hard points. Her femininity screamed with sensation.

''Maddie...Maddie...Maddie...'' Dylan increased the tempo, hammering into her, murmuring earthy, erotic words, telling her explicitly what he wanted and what he felt.

Throbbing unbearably, the need for fulfillment rioting inside her, Maddie gasped and panted while Dylan's hard, powerful lunges took her to the very edge. And then with one final thrust, he flung her into a moaning, clawing explosion of the senses unequaled by any other experience in her life. While her climax burst inside her, around her and through her, Maddie felt his release jet into her, strong and hot. Dylan cried out, hammered frenetically into her several times, then grunted as he buried his head against her shoulder.

Maddie slid her legs down his hips and over his legs until her feet touched the floor. But he clasped her hips, keeping their bodies molded together and his sex inside her. When she lifted her gaze to look at him, he lowered his head, whispered, ''Sweet Maddie,'' and kissed her again.

Eleven

Dylan woke Maddie before dawn. He wanted her again. Needed her in such a desperate way that he felt frightened. He had lost control last night, when he'd taken her so savagely downstairs in the living room, totally forgetting about protection for the first time since he'd become sexually active. But even now, hours afterward, he knew if he had it to do over again, he would still be powerless to change what had happened, to do anything differently. The overwhelming hunger to take Maddie had turned him into nothing more than a male animal ruled completely by the instinct to mate. As he lay beside her in his bed, in his boyhood bedroom, he watched while she slept, cuddled against him. Peacefully. And so trusting. He'd never felt such a strong desire to possess and protect a woman. There was nothing lukewarm, nothing insignificant, nothing halfway about his feelings for Maddie. She was his now, whether she knew it or not. She belonged to him in the most basic, elemental way a woman could belong to a man.

He leaned over and kissed her naked shoulder. She sighed. Illumination from the streetlight outside mixed with the moonlight so he could see her quite plainly. He lowered the sheet and blanket covering her and eased them down until he revealed her round, full breasts. Her body was lush and sexy, every inch a true work of art. Tiny freckles dotted her shoulders, and a small red mole kissed the cleavage between her breasts. Her nipples were large and rosy, the aureoles a shade lighter. He skimmed his fingertips over her collarbone. She stirred, whimpering in her sleep. Lifting the covers, he flung them to the foot of the bed, leaving Maddie totally exposed. His sex thrust forward, hard and ready. But this time he would be more careful. Rising from the bed, he glimpsed her as she turned over and curled into a fetal ball, her body obviously seeking warmth. He hurried into the bathroom, rummaged through his shaving kit until he found the pack of three condoms that he kept there for emergencies whenever he traveled. They were at least two years old.

When he returned to the bed, already sheathed and ready to make love, he called her name softly. No response. Dylan crawled into bed behind her, drew her body close to his, her back to his chest, and nuzzled her neck.

"Maddie?"

She sighed. "Hmmm..."

"I want you."

She sighed again. "Mmm."

While kissing her neck, he eased one hand over her

waist and reached up to tweak first one nipple and then the other.

She moaned. "Dylan?"

He moved his hand over her belly and down to her mound, then slipped his fingers between her thighs and rubbed her intimately.

"Wake up, honey." Stroking her feminine nub, he brought her to life, and when she tried to turn over, he held her in place.

"Dylan, I—"

He lifted one of her legs, parting her thighs, and took her from behind. He entered her, then withdrew quickly and repeated the bold thrust.

"Damn, Maddie, you feel so good. So hot and wet." He shuddered. "I'm so hungry for you."

Maddie rocked her hips back and forth, encouraging him to continue. "Love me, Dylan. Love me some more."

That was all the encouragement he needed. He pumped into her, loving the feel of burying himself in her receptive body. But soon she wriggled and whimpered, her hands grasping behind her to touch him, her nails raking down his hip and thigh.

"Want something?" he asked, suddenly ceasing his movements.

"Yes."

"Tell me what you want." He nipped her shoulder.

She shivered. "You know what I want."

"Yes, I know."

He slipped his left arm beneath her and brought his hand up to her breast, while he eased his other hand over her mound and dipped his fingers between her wet, swollen lips. When he massaged her, she bucked against his hand. With his fingers working feverishly to excite her, he resumed his deep, hard thrusts; then he nuzzled her hair away from her neck, lowered his mouth and licked her warm, salty skin.

Feeling her tightening around his fingers, Dylan increased the speed and the pressure until her back arched and she bowed with tension; then suddenly she moaned as fulfillment claimed her. While she shivered and shook with pleasure, he shattered with a release so powerful and complete. A distinct ringing echoed in his ears, and satiation spread through his body as the aftershocks continued long past the initial blast.

Later, when they were both half-asleep, Maddie turned in his arms until she faced him. "I love making love with you," she said.

"Ditto." He kissed her.

Laying her head on his shoulder, she cuddled up against him and within minutes fell asleep.

They made love again at daybreak and later shortly before eight, then showered together. Dylan took a pair of jeans out of the closet, slipped into them and looked at Maddie standing there with a towel wrapped around her.

"My clothes are downstairs," she reminded him.

He jerked a chambray shirt off a hanger and tossed it to her. ''Here, honey, make do with this until we can gather up your stuff.''

Smiling at him, she caught the shirt in midair. ''I've never been so deliciously sore and exhausted,'' she told him.

He grinned. ''Did I wear you out, Red?''

She dropped the towel. He leered at her and she giggled. ''How long has it been since you did it four times in eight hours?''

He surveyed her from head to toe. ''If you don't cover up, it's going to be five times.''

Maddie leisurely slipped into the oversize shirt, the hem hitting her mid-thigh and the long sleeves covering her hands. She buttoned the shirt and rolled up the sleeves. ''There. Is that better?''

''Not better, but a heck of a lot less tempting.'' He reached out and dragged her into his arms. With his face lowered to hers, he said, ''I haven't been so horny since I was twenty. And I've never wanted another woman the way I want you.''

She closed her eyes and sighed. ''I feel the same.''

He kissed her forehead, her closed eyelids and then her mouth. ''You've never wanted another woman the way you want me?'' he asked jokingly.

Her eyelids opened wide as she gasped, then she giggled again. ''Crazy man! You know what I meant.'' She wrapped her arms around his neck. ''I've never felt this way about any other man. Only you.''

"It's good between us, Maddie. Really good."

"Yes, it is."

"The best ever."

"Dylan?"

"Mmm-hmm?"

"I—"

The doorbell rang. Why now? Why not five minutes from now, after she'd told Dylan she loved him? The sex had been incredible, but what she felt for him went beyond sex. It was love. Love unlike any she'd ever experienced.

"I'd better get that," he told her.

"While you see who it is, I'll gather up my clothes from the living room."

"Good idea. How about getting mine while you're at it?"

She nodded. He disappeared out the door. Maddie went back into the bathroom, found a comb, raked it through her damp hair and took a good look at herself in the mirror. Her lips were swollen, she had a small bruise on her neck and one cheek was red from where Dylan's beard had scraped her flesh. She knew there were similar red patches on her breasts and her inner thighs.

Maddie sighed as her body recalled the pleasure. How could anything be so absolutely wonderful? She hugged herself and whirled around and around. She was in love, in love, in love.

Savoring the sweetness of the emotions bubbling

over inside her, Maddie padded barefoot down the stairs, but halted when she reached the foyer. She heard voices. Dylan's and Hart's. Oh, drat. Where were they? Surely Dylan hadn't taken Hart into the living room where their discarded clothes lay strewn all over the place. Tiptoeing quietly toward the living room, she realized the voices came from the study. She released a relieved sigh. If Hart discovered that she and Dylan had become lovers, he would tell Joan and then Maddie would have some explaining to do to her best friend. It wasn't that she didn't plan to tell Joan. She did. But not right now. Everything was so new and wonderful and unbelievably good that she didn't want to share it with anyone. Not yet.

Hurriedly Maddie dashed into the living room and item by item gathered up their clothing. She found both of Dylan's shoes, but only one of hers, so she dumped the pile of clothing and accessories on the sofa and crawled around on the floor until she spotted her shoe in the magazine rack. How in the world had it gotten there?

Just as she picked up the clothes, stacked both pairs of shoes on top of her bundle and headed for the stairs, Hart came out of the study, Dylan rushing behind him.

"Hart, wait up," Dylan said.

"Well, good morning, Maddie," Hart said. "You're looking rather fetching. Is that some new kind of fashion fad?"

With an armful of clothes, Maddie squared her

shoulders, tilted her chin and turned around to face her best friend's husband. "Ha, ha. Very funny."

Hart grinned sheepishly. "I just dropped by to tell you that we caught up with those guys who threatened you last night." His smile vanished as he glanced over his shoulder at Dylan. "They crashed their car during the chase. Both of the guys are in the hospital in pretty bad shape."

"Oh." Maddie didn't know how to feel or how to react.

"I hate to say this, but if they work for whom we think they do, then they'll go to the pen before they'll talk," Hart said.

"Hart thinks you need a bodyguard," Dylan said. "And I agree."

"What?" Were they kidding? No, she could tell by the serious looks on their faces that they were not kidding. "I thought you were providing police protection. Isn't that enough?"

"I'm afraid there's no way we can spare a couple of guys to keep watch over you and Dylan twenty-four seven. And unless Dylan does hop the next plane back to Dallas, there could be more threats and probably—"

"Are you going back to Dallas?" Maddie looked at Dylan.

"No, but—"

"Good. We can't let them make us run scared."

Dylan's lips twitched in an almost smile. "Us?"

She shrugged. ''Yes, us.''

''Don't argue with her,'' Hart said. ''Just hire her a bodyguard.''

Dylan walked Hart to the front door. ''Let us know what happens with those two guys in the hospital. Maddie is going to press charges. I want you to throw the book at them.'' Dylan opened the door and Hart stepped out onto the porch. ''And whatever you do, don't let me get anywhere near them.''

''Yeah, I know just how you feel,'' Hart said. ''The same way I'd feel if somebody threatened Joan.''

Maddie met Dylan just as he closed the front door. Startled by her unexpected nearness, Dylan jerked back from her.

''I can fix breakfast after I get dressed,'' she said.

''I think I should take you home and stay with you until we can round up a bodyguard for you.''

''What about a bodyguard for you?''

''I can take care of myself.''

''And I can't, is that it?'' She glared at him.

''Not after what happened last night.''

''I'm not the one who got hit in the head and suffered a concussion.''

Dylan winced. ''A mild concussion.''

''But I'm—''

''Stop arguing and get dressed.''

She glanced at his naked chest and bare feet. ''What about you? Are you going out like that?''

"You're very argumentative in the mornings, aren't you?"

"Only when I don't get my way."

"Only when you..." Dylan laughed. "God, Maddie, you're priceless."

"Actually, I'm not," she replied. "I'm worth three point five billion dollars."

Dylan reached out, took the stack of clothes and shoes from her, dumped them on the floor and pulled her into his arms. With his nose touching hers, he said, "Your net worth might be in the billions, but you, sweet Maddie, are priceless."

Tears misted her eyes. Heaven help her if he was lying to her, because she believed him with her whole heart. "You're just saying that because you want to get in my pants."

Dylan slid his hands up and under the chambray shirt and cupped her naked buttocks. "You aren't wearing any."

"Oh." She looked at him point-blank. "Then that should make it easier for you, shouldn't it?"

Dylan grinned wickedly, then walked her backward into the living room and toppled her onto the sofa. He unzipped his jeans, freed his jutting sex and came down over her. Maddie spread her legs apart and held open her arms in welcome.

Dylan didn't take Maddie to her condo and she didn't go to work. After calling Alicia and giving her a synopsis of last night's events, Maddie spent the day in Dylan's arms. They ate cold cereal for breakfast at eleven, then munched on peanut butter and crackers for a late three-o'clock lunch. Finally around four, they showered again and Dylan dressed in slacks and a short-sleeved cotton shirt. While Maddie pressed the rumpled skirt she'd worn to work yesterday, Dylan made some phone calls. He intended to find the best security agency in Texas and hire their most qualified bodyguard for Maddie.

He couldn't tuck tail and run back to Dallas. But he couldn't risk Maddie's life either. As he studied the telephone number his lawyer had given him, he thought about the fact that the richest woman in Texas had been going about her business for years without a bodyguard, and here she was waist-deep in trouble because of him and needing a hulking protector to keep her safe. He supposed he should talk things over with her before he made the call. Maybe Maddie had a preference. Dylan knew that he did. He'd like a female bodyguard for Maddie.

"Damn lovesick fool," he mumbled to himself. "You can't stand the thought of another man getting that close to her, can you?"

Just as Dylan headed out of the study to find Maddie, the phone rang. He turned around, went over to his father's desk and picked up the receiver.

"Dylan Bridges."

"Hello, Mr. Bridges," a quiet, muffled voice said.

Dylan tensed. Another warning? "What do you want?" Anger flared inside him.

"I've got to make this quick, in case your phone is tapped."

"What? My phone's— Who is this?"

"I can see to it that the murder weapon that disappeared from the crime lab gets back in police hands."

"Did you take the gun?"

"Don't talk. Just listen. If you want the gun and information about the man who killed your father, then we can make a deal. Are you interested?"

Damn, just who was he dealing with here? Dylan wondered. A member of the mob? A crooked cop? "I'm interested."

"It'll cost you."

"How much?"

"First we bargain for the gun. I want fifty thousand for the gun. If that goes off without a hitch, then we'll bargain for the information."

"All right. Fifty thousand. When and where do I meet you?"

"You don't. I'll call you back in thirty minutes and tell you where to bring the money. Tonight. If I get my money, I'll return the gun."

"How do I know I can trust you?"

The dial tone hummed in Dylan's ear. Damn!

Looking neat as a pin, Maddie appeared in the doorway. "What's wrong? Was that bad news?"

Dylan hung up the phone. "I just got a call from a guy who says he has the murder weapon that was stolen from the crime lab. He says that for enough money, he'll return the gun."

"Call Hart right now and—"

"No! If this guy's on the up and up, I don't want to do anything that might scare him off," Dylan said. "If he's a crooked cop, he might find out if I get in touch with Hart."

"What are you going to do?"

"I'm going to wait for the guy to call back in thirty minutes to tell me when and where to drop off the money." Dylan motioned her to come into the study. "In the meantime, I'm going to get in touch with—" he picked up the paper on which he'd written the security agency's number "—the Leighton Security Agency in Houston and get them to send us a bodyguard." His gaze connected with hers. "Would you prefer a female bodyguard?"

"A woman? I hadn't thought about it, but…yes, I'd prefer a woman. If I have to spend twenty-four hours a day with someone, it might be easier if that someone is another woman."

"Yeah, that's just what I thought." Dylan grinned. "Let me see what I can do. We need her here ASAP. If this guy wants me to make the drop tonight, I have no intention of leaving you alone while I'm gone."

"How much money does he want?" Maddie asked.

"Fifty thousand."

"I can get that for you with one phone call to—"

"I don't need your money, Red. I can have it transferred from my bank today."

"Why can't I go with you tonight or whenever you're told to make the drop?" Maddie sashayed up to him and slipped her arms around his neck. "My bodyguard and I can come along to guard you."

"No way." He removed her arms from around his neck, then grasped her chin. "I'm not going to put you in the line of fire."

"But, Dylan—"

He squeezed her chin. "No!" Before she could do more than glare at him, he lifted the phone and dialed the Houston number.

Maddie paced the floor in the living room of her condo. Six foot, one hundred and seventy-five pound Geraldine "Gerri" Nightingale sat on the sofa watching Maddie. Her bodyguard had the build of a linebacker, only in smaller proportions, and a round cherubic face that belied her forty years. She wore her chestnut brown hair in a short, stylish bob that showed her ears and revealed a pair of tiny gold hoops. She dressed casually in black slacks and a tan jacket that concealed the big 9mm gun strapped to her hip. And her keen brown eyes seemed to have the ability to see right, left, forward and backward—all at the same time.

''It's been over an hour. Where is he?'' Maddie glared at Gerri. ''We should have followed him.''

''Mr. Bridges requested that we remain here.''

''Screw Mr. Bridges' request.'' Maddie knew her behavior bordered on childish, but she was worried sick about Dylan. The damn fool man had gone off with fifty thousand dollars in a navy blue gym bag. On his way where? He had refused to give her any information. Just the thought that something bad might happen to Dylan kept Maddie's stomach churning. She couldn't lose him. In only a few short weeks, he'd come to mean everything to her.

''Ms. Delarue, why don't you sit down and relax,'' Gerri said. ''I'm sure Mr. Bridges will phone you as soon as he finishes conducting his business.''

''Very dangerous business. He could be walking into a trap. At least if we'd followed him, he'd have backup.'' Maddie eyed Gerri's holster, half hidden by her open jacket. ''Just how good are you with that?'' Maddie nodded toward the gun.

''I never miss,'' Gerri said.

''See, if we'd followed him and he got into trouble, you could have...you could have shot somebody.''

''Yes, ma'am.''

Maddie continued her pacing. Call, dammit, Dylan. Call!

''Mind if I catch the ten-o'clock news?'' Gerri asked.

''What?''

"May I turn on the TV?"

"Sure, go ahead."

Gerri punched the remote control and the huge flat screen television came on instantly. While Maddie's bodyguard flipped through the stations, the telephone rang.

Maddie made a mad dash to the phone, grabbed the receiver and said "Hello."

"Hi, Red."

"Oh, God, Dylan, where are you? How are you?"

"I'm on my way to your place," he replied. "And I'm fine."

"How did it go?"

"As far as I know, it went okay. I left the gym bag on the seat of the third booth on the left at Coyote Harry's and I picked up the menu and found a note, just like thc guy had told me."

"If you'd called Hart—"

"Then our guy wouldn't have picked up the cash," Dylan said. "If he's a cop, then he'd have smelled a setup and he'd have recognized any undercover people the police would have stationed at the restaurant."

"All right. It's done now. So what does the note say?"

"It's better if you don't know."

"At least tell me when you make the next exchange."

"If the gun reappears as promised, then I meet the guy tomorrow night for the information."

''So soon?''

''The sooner the better. This guy could give me enough information for the police to arrest my father's murderer.''

''But what if—'' She swallowed, barely able to form the thought let alone voice it aloud. ''What if he's setting you up? What if when you get there, it's a trap and they—?''

''I won't go into this blind,'' Dylan said. ''I'll be very careful. Now, stop worrying and put on something really sexy. I'll be there in about fifteen minutes.''

''Did you forget that I now have a shadow that follows me everywhere?''

''She's not going to follow you to bed tonight, is she?''

''She certainly isn't. She'll be sleeping in the guest bedroom.''

''That's good to know. I'm not really into threesomes.''

''Threesomes?'' Maddie gasped, then sighed when the implication became clear to her. ''Does that mean you plan to stay here tonight?''

''Yeah, honey, that's exactly what it means. And for your information, I do intend to follow you to bed.''

Twelve

Totally naked, Maddie crawled out of bed quietly, keeping a sleeping Dylan in her peripheral vision as she sneaked across the room. She lifted Dylan's sport coat off the chair where he'd placed it last night, then delved her hand into the inside pocket. All the coercing in the world hadn't persuaded Dylan to tell her when and where he would meet the informant tonight—and she was damned and determined to find out. Once she knew the particulars, she could follow him, at a discreet distance, of course; and she'd take Gerri Nightingale and her big gun along with her.

Maddie removed the hand-printed note, scanned it quickly, then replaced it inside Dylan's jacket. The rodeo arena, outside of town. Eleven o'clock tonight. Undoubtedly there were no events scheduled tonight, so the place would be deserted. A quiet, private meeting area, with only one road in and out, easy to check for a setup. But anyone could come in afterward or get there hours before to set up an ambush.

Dylan turned over and groaned. Maddie laid his jacket exactly where it had been, then tiptoed toward the bed. Dylan groaned again, reached out and ran his hand over her side of the king-size bed. She made it halfway back to bed before he opened his eyes and looked around the bed and then around the room.

"What are you doing way over there?" As he rose into a sitting position, the sheet dropped to his waist, revealing a broad chest, dusted with curly brown hair, a washboard-lean belly and large muscular biceps. Fully clothed, Dylan Bridges was drop-dead gorgeous. Naked, the man had no equal.

"I...uh...I was trying to be quiet so I wouldn't wake you." She stood in the middle of her huge bedroom suite, naked and not the least embarrassed. After all, Dylan had seen every inch of her. Actually he'd touched and tasted every inch of her.

"Just where were you going like that?" As he scanned her from head to toe, his gaze lingered on her breasts.

Maddie giggled nervously. "I was going to hop in the shower, then—"

"Why don't you come back to bed?" He patted the empty place on her side of the bed, then reached over on the nightstand to remove a condom from the box he'd purchased yesterday.

"You have a one-track mind, Mr. Bridges." She sauntered toward the bed, letting her hips sway provocatively.

As she neared the edge of the bed, she said, "Morning, noon and night, all you think about is sex."

He reached out, grabbed her wrist and dragged her

toward him across the rumpled sheets. She went willingly, assisting him gladly. He kicked the covers to the foot of the bed, hauled her up and on top of him. She straddled his hips and pressed her femininity against his erection.

"How about a hard, fast ride on a bucking bronc?" He caressed her naked buttocks.

"Sounds like the perfect way to start the day." After lifting herself up on her knees, she positioned her body, reached down, circled his sex and drew him up and into her. She slid over him, easing the width and length into her sheath. When she had taken him fully inside her, she moved up and down, placing the friction of their rubbing bodies precisely where it aroused her. Easing forward so that her breasts rested near his mouth, Maddie smiled at Dylan.

He lifted his head, opened his mouth and took one begging nipple between his lips. Maddie moaned. He shifted back and forth from one breast to the other, one sensitive tip to the other. And all the while he rubbed her hips and buttocks, gently guiding her.

She rode him at a steady pace, allowing the tension to build gradually, but eventually the sensations grew so intense that she lost control. Riding him harder and faster, she pounded frenetically until the vibrations screeched and clawed and exploded, sending shockwaves through her body. When her climax tapered off to tingling remnants, she fell limply on top of him. Dylan kissed and stroked her as the eruptions subsided, then he flipped her onto her back and hovered over her. While she lay beneath him, drowsily sated, he took her fully, completely and found his own release after several quick, hard thrusts. He shuddered and shook, then collapsed on top of her.

Maddie thought she heard the telephone ringing, but a blissfully sweet buzz still hummed inside her head. A loud knock on the bedroom door aroused her from the dreamy aftermath.

"Maddie," Thelma Hewitt called. "Telephone for Mr. Bridges. It's Detective O'Brien."

Dylan rolled off Maddie and onto the bed. "Thanks, Thelma," Dylan said.

"Oh, and by the way, Gerri is eating breakfast. She loves my chocolate chip pancakes, and there's enough for everybody."

"We'll be there in a few minutes." Dylan scooted to the side of the bed, reached over and lifted the receiver from the brass-and-crystal French telephone. "Bridges here."

Maddie slid across the bed, came up on her knees behind Dylan and, pressing her breasts against his back, draped her arms around his neck.

"Yeah, how about that?" Dylan swatted at Maddie's playful fingers twisting and twining his chest hair. "Who knows? Uh-huh. Thanks for calling, Hart."

The minute he replaced the receiver, he yanked

Maddie off his back and into his arms. Giggling, she stared at him mischievously.

"Why did Hart call?" she asked.

"To tell me that the gun that disappeared from the crime lab has miraculously reappeared."

Maddie sobered, her playful attitude dissolving into seriousness. "Which means you're going to meet that guy tonight and give him another fifty thousand, doesn't it?"

"That was our deal," Dylan said. "I give him fifty thousand and he returns the gun. That's been accomplished. Now he'll meet with me and for another fifty thousand, he'll give me the information I need to prove who killed my father."

"And you won't let me go with you?"

"Absolutely not."

"And you won't tell Hart and let him—"

"We've been over this before, honey. No police. I'm not taking any chances of scaring off this guy. I think he's nervous, probably frightened of the killer."

"How do you know that he's not the person who killed the judge? Maybe, for some reason, he wants to kill you, too."

Dylan kissed her, then lifted her to her feet as he stood. "Put on some clothes. I'm hungry for Thelma's chocolate chip pancakes."

He had dismissed her concerns as if they were nothing, but she knew better. All right, let him go off by himself to the rendezvous at the rodeo arena tonight at eleven. She had every intention of being there no more than five minutes behind him. She and Gerri and Gerri's gun.

After promising to phone her the minute his meeting with the mysterious informant ended, Dylan left Maddie's condo around nine, money-filled gym bag in tow, then drove to his father's house on Royal Avenue. Just in case Maddie decided to follow him, he wanted to catch her well in advance of the actual meeting. But much to his relief, he saw no signs of being followed by anyone. He stayed at the house, watching some special documentary on the animal channel about the vanishing mustangs in the American West. At ten-thirty, he locked up, got in his rental car and headed out of town.

Although the road leading up to the rodeo arena and barns was dark, the arena itself was well-lit. He parked the car, removed the gym bag and made his way around toward the back gate, the arranged rendezvous spot. A hundred grand would be a small price to pay if it bought him the name of the bastard who'd killed his father. With a name and the right information, the police could bring the guy in for questioning—and check his palm print against the one they'd found on the murder weapon. And it would be all the better if the person he was meeting could throw in a little substantial evidence, along with a name and the info.

The back gate lay in shadows, but there was enough

light for Dylan to check his watch. Ten-fifty. He was early.

Minutes dragged by, each seeming like a hour. Finally Dylan heard the roar of a car's motor. His heartbeat thundered inside his head. He felt inside his jacket pocket for the fifteen-round 9mm Ruger that he'd kept in the glove compartment of his Porsche. He'd like to think that he wouldn't need a weapon, but he wasn't fool enough to walk into a situation like this unarmed. He had no idea what type of person he was dealing with or what the outcome of their meeting might be.

Vigilant, on alert and psyching himself up for whatever happened, Dylan waited. A couple of minutes before ten, a short, wiry man in his late twenties crept around the fence, but hesitated a good thirty feet away from Dylan. From what Dylan could make out in the semidarkness and from the distance between them, the man appeared to be Hispanic. But when he spoke, he had no accent.

"You got the money?" the guy called.

Dylan lifted the gym bag and stuck it out in front of him.

The man glanced nervously all around him. "You came alone like I told you to do, didn't you?"

"I'm all alone," Dylan replied.

"Put the gym bag down and kick it toward me."

"Before I get my information?"

"I get the money, then you get the information."

Dylan nodded. The hairs on the back of his neck stood straight up. Something wasn't right. He could feel it in his gut. He hesitated and listened, but heard nothing. Still, he sensed trouble.

"What are you waiting for?" the guy yelled.

"Did you come alone?" Dylan rubbed his hand over his jacket. The Ruger was only a second away, if he needed it. Thank God he knew how to use a gun. When he and a couple of Dallas business associates had taken up target practice as a way to relieve work-related tension, Dylan had never imagined the day would come when he might be forced to defend himself with a pistol.

"Hell, man, you think I'd bring along somebody? I'm trying to get enough money to get away...far away from Mission Creek and the guy who hired me to steal the gun he used to kill your papa."

"What man hired you? And just who are you? How were you able to take a gun from a police crime lab?"

"I don't answer no questions. Not before I get my money."

Dylan set the gym bag on the ground, then kicked it forward a good five feet.

"Now, you back up," the man told him. "And keep backing up until I tell you to stop."

Dylan obeyed, and while he was backing away, he sensed danger all around him. The man made his way slowly and cautiously toward the gym bag. He kept glancing right and left, as if he expected to be jumped at any minute. Dylan understood the guy's fears; he was pretty jittery himself.

Just as the guy reached down for the gym bag, Dylan heard a sound. A couple of seconds later he realized what he'd heard. A gunshot. The bullet ripped through the nighttime quiet and hit its mark, straight into the informant's chest. Dylan dove behind a huge, metal Dumpster, yanked the Ruger from his jacket and waited. Footsteps. Breathing. God, maybe it was his own breathing he heard. But the footsteps were coming closer.

"You're next, Bridges," a voice said. "We were both idiots to trust that son of a bitch Torrez. I paid him a thousand bucks to retrieve my Sig and what does he do when I tell him to take it to Corpus Christi and dump it in the Gulf? He keeps it and sells it to you. Lucky for me that I got buddies everywhere, keeping their eyes and ears open. And even luckier for me that Torrez's whore was more afraid of me than of him."

Whoever this guy was he was a cocky bastard. But he wasn't completely stupid. He hadn't shown himself. And he'd suddenly gotten awfully quiet. Did that mean he was moving toward Dylan? Was there any way he could get behind him?

Dylan heard another noise. A car? Damn, if this guy had arranged for backup, Dylan was in trouble.

"You got help coming?" the man asked, and Dylan realized the guy was still in front of him somewhere and that whoever had just driven up to the arena wasn't working for the enemy.

"Could be." But who? Dylan wondered. Could Maddie have called Hart and told him— Told him what? She didn't know the details of this meeting.

Dylan glanced all around him. Two shadows, one tall and one short, appeared from the right, and they were getting closer and closer. Whoever it was, they were walking directly into the line of fire.

Then everything happened at once. He recognized the late arrivals: Maddie Delarue, with her bodyguard at her side. Her gun drawn, Gerri was ready to fire. Just as Dylan started to yell out a warning, the guy who'd already shot one person tonight fired his weapon, which missed its target. Gerri Nightingale knocked Maddie out of the way and took the gunman's second bullet. Maddie screamed. Dylan ran out of hiding when Gerri hit the ground, firing his Ruger repeatedly and racing toward Maddie. He had to get her out of harm's way. Damn it, what the hell was she doing here? How had she known where he'd be?

Just as Dylan reached out to grab Maddie, the gunman got off another shot. One that hit its target.

Thirteen

Being rich enough to buy just about everything and everyone in Mission Creek had its advantages. Being able to promise huge endowments to the hospital opened doors for Maddie, allowing her privileges often denied others. She had kept a vigil at Dylan's bedside in the surgical intensive care unit after a bullet had been removed from his shoulder, although visitors weren't generally allowed except at posted times throughout the day. And twelve hours later, when the doctors deemed it safe, Maddie had Dylan moved into the deluxe suite at Mission Creek Memorial. Decorated more like an elegant bedroom with an attached sitting room, the suite boasted cherry furniture, a camelback sofa that made out into a double bed and two Queen Anne wing chairs, as well as a small cherry table and two straight-back chairs for dining.

As Maddie sat at Dylan's bedside watching him devour his first substantial meal—prepared and delivered by Thelma Hewitt—she thanked God for the millionth time that Dylan's injuries hadn't been fatal. No thanks to her. He'd been shot trying to protect her. She felt like a complete idiot, which of course she was. But even Dylan agreed that when all was said and done, she'd done the right thing. By that he had not meant her following him to the rodeo arena; he'd meant her last-minute phone call to Hart.

When she'd called Dylan a hero, he'd said gruffly, "Hart O'Brien is the real hero. Phoning him was a smart move, Maddie. If he hadn't shown up when he did..."

Maddie didn't want to think about what would have happened if Hart hadn't arrived at the rodeo arena, along with four other police officers, only minutes after both Dylan and Gerri had been shot.

"Stop frowning, Red," Dylan said. "Your face might freeze like that."

She offered him a feeble smile. "Hart phoned while you were in the bathroom. He's coming over."

"Big news? Why don't you go ahead and tell me what you know?" With his good arm Dylan pushed his empty plate to the side of the portable tray, then shoved the tray away from the bed. His left shoulder was heavily bandaged and his arm taped to his chest.

"If I had my way, Hart would wait until you're fully recovered to—"

"I took a slug in the shoulder," Dylan said. "I'll be as good as new in a week or so. Honey, you've got to stop trying to protect me from the world, from anything that might be the slightest bit unpleasant. I'm a grown man. Big and strong. Or at least getting stronger by the minute. And I'm mostly in my right mind. I don't need a caretaker."

Maddie nodded. When tears welled up in her eyes, she turned away from him.

Dylan grabbed her wrist. "I don't need a caretaker. But I need a friend...and a lover."

She turned back to him, tears trickling down her face, and forced herself to smile.

"I do need you, sweet Maddie." He tugged on her wrist; she eased toward the bed. "I just don't need you to be my mother or my nurse or my bodyguard. Understand?"

She nodded.

"Speaking of bodyguards, how's Gerri today?" he asked.

"She's still in intensive care, but they're hoping to move her into a private room tomorrow."

When Dylan tugged again, she moved closer. He released her and patted the side of the bed. She sat down beside him, being careful not to jostle him. He circled her waist with his arm.

"I want you to stop blaming yourself for what happened to Gerri and me," Dylan told her.

"Whom should I blame?"

"Blame fate. Blame me. Blame the guy who tried to kill us. But do not blame yourself."

"But I'm the one who nearly got us—" Tears lodged in her throat.

"You thought you were doing the right thing. Actually by calling Hart, you saved all our lives. And if I'd been smart, I'd have contacted Hart when I received that first phone call. You tried to convince me to let the police in on what was going on.''

She gazed at him lovingly. ''Here you are recuperating from a gunshot wound, lying in a hospital bed, and you're the one comforting me. Don't we have our roles reversed?''

''Nah.'' He grinned. ''Comforting is a two-way street. You've been doing your share lately.'' Dylan slipped his hand around the back of her neck and urged her downward until her lips hovered over his. ''How long do we have before Hart shows up?'' he asked, his lips brushing hers as he spoke.

Maddie sucked in her breath. ''You're in no shape for any hanky-panky. Besides, Hart's due any minute now.''

The suite door opened. ''Hart's here, so whatever you two were about to do will have to wait.''

Dylan chuckled. ''I was just trying to talk Nurse Maddie into giving me a sponge bath.''

Hart grinned. ''She can clean you up later. But for now I thought you might want me to bring you up to date on several items of interest.''

Maddie eased off the bed and into a nearby chair. Hart stood at the foot of the bed.

''Shoot,'' Dylan said, then winced and chuckled. ''Poor choice of words.''

''Well, our shooter—a Mr. Alex Black—is behind

bars. Arrested for the murder of Carl Bridges and the murder of Manuel Torrez, the guy who stole the gun from the crime lab."

"How did you know? What proof do y'all have?" Dylan asked. "Will it stand up in court?"

"Manuel Torrez, a member of the janitorial staff who cleans all the city buildings, including the crime lab, stole the gun for Black, but he got greedy and thought he'd make enough money to skip town by selling the gun's return and information to you." Hart glanced at Maddie. "You two should have called me when that guy first contacted you."

"Yeah, hindsight is twenty-twenty," Dylan said.

"Well, Torrez lived long enough to finger Black as the guy who'd hired him to steal the gun and—" Hart paused for effect "—Black's palm print matches the one found on the murder weapon."

"I'll be damned." Dylan shook his head. "Has this guy—this Alex Black—explained why he killed my father?"

"He's denying he did it, but we've got him and he's not slipping through the cracks. I promise you that we'll get a conviction." Hart looked right at Dylan. "Black is a two-bit hood, with ties to the mob. Take my word for it, the guy's going down."

Dylan held out his hand. Hart rounded the bed and the two men shook hands. "Thanks," Dylan said. "Thanks for everything."

"Just doing my job."

"Yeah, well, I didn't make it easy for you, did I? Sorry about that."

Hart shrugged. "For you, it was personal. Under similar circumstances, I might have done the same thing."

"I need to know why," Dylan said. "There has to be a reason. Somebody hired Alex Black to kill my father."

"It may take us awhile to find out who and why, but sooner or later we'll nail whoever was behind the hit." Hart placed his hand on Dylan's shoulder. "How about leaving the rest to us? Let the police handle things from here on out."

"Yeah, I'll do that."

Hart turned to Maddie. "Keep him out of trouble, will you?"

"Me?" Maddie pointed to her chest. "He doesn't listen to me. I have no control over him whatsoever."

Hart grinned, then glanced at Dylan. "She'll eventually figure it out and when she does, you're a goner." Hart pointed his finger at Dylan and clicked his tongue as he jerked his finger mimicking a gun firing. "And when that happens, it'll kick you on your ass a lot worse than a gunshot."

When Hart left, Maddie looked quizzically at Dylan. "What on earth was he talking about?"

"Beats me." Dylan shrugged.

Five days later, Maddie brought Dylan to her condo and spent the next few days waiting on him hand and foot. She was driving him nuts, but he'd given up trying to stop her, because she thought of playing nursemaid as part of her penance. She'd taken all the blame in what went wrong, when in fact, he'd been more to blame than anyone else. Hell, if he hadn't been so cocksure of himself, so damned and determined to solve the murder case and not share info with Hart O'Brien, he might not have almost gotten Maddie and Gerri and himself killed.

Other than having a mighty sore shoulder, he felt okay. He really didn't need Maddie buzzing around him, doing everything for him, but no matter what he said, she didn't listen. What he wanted—what he needed—was to make love to Maddie. But she considered him an invalid and whenever he put the moves on her, she scolded him and reminded him of his condition. Hell, she'd even put him in the guest bedroom!

When he entered the kitchen at ten after eight, he was surprised not to see Maddie waiting for him. Instead he found only Thelma busily emptying the dishwasher.

"Morning," she said. "Sleep well?"

"Slept okay," he replied. "Where's Maddie?"

"Still asleep. That child has worn herself to a frazzle lately. I doubt she'd gotten more than two or three hours sleep a night since you got shot."

"I've been out of the hospital and here with her for three nights, why hasn't she—"

"She gets up every couple of hours and checks on you."

Dylan huffed. "What can I do to convince her I'm practically a hundred percent again?"

"It'll have to be something dramatic," Thelma said. "And I'd suggest something romantic."

"Romantic, huh?"

"You don't want to spend the next few weeks living like a monk, do you?"

Dylan blushed. He wasn't accustomed to discussing his love life with anyone, least of all his lover's housekeeper.

"Maddie adores the ballet, and one of our local Mission Creek gals is a prima ballerina with the Houston Ballet. Why don't you take Maddie into Houston for a night out? Show her how well you are and romance her at the same time."

"Mmm-hmm. Thelma, you're a genius."

"I'm not a genius, just a very observant, intuitive woman. And I know Maddie."

"The ballet, a limousine, dinner at a five-star restaurant...a perfect way to say goodbye."

Thelma glared at him. "What do you mean a perfect way to say goodbye?"

"I'll soon be fully recovered and I've agreed to let the police handle everything concerning my father's murder from here on out. It's time I head back to Dallas, to my job and my life there."

"What about Maddie?"

"What about her?"

"Are you just going to run off and leave her?"

"I'm not running off," Dylan said in self-defense. "I'm going home. Maddie and I are friends. I hope we remain friends and—" He'd almost said "and lovers." "But we agreed, going into our relationship, that we're both lousy at commitments, at anything permanent."

"And you don't think maybe, just maybe, things might be different with Maddie?"

"Things are different with Maddie. We're not going to hurt each other. We're going to remain friends."

Did he truly believe what he was saying? Could he be nothing more than a friend to Maddie? Hell, no, not when every instinct within him longed to be her lover. But he'd screwed up Maddie's life more than once. How could he be sure he wouldn't do it again? He couldn't risk it, didn't dare reach out and grab the one thing he wanted most in this world—Maddie Delarue, his woman for the rest of their lives.

Besides, would she or anyone else ever believe that a business shark like Dylan Bridges hadn't married her for her money?

Thelma continued glaring at him, then she slammed the dishwasher door and walked straight up to him.

"Dylan Bridges, you're a damn fool. That's what you are."

He leaned over and kissed Thelma on both cheeks and said, "And you, Ms. Hewitt, are an old romantic who believes in happily-ever-after endings. But Maddie and I are smart enough not to expect fairy-tale endings for our lives."

"I said it once and I'll say it again. Dylan Bridges, you're a damn fool!"

Maddie stood outside the kitchen door, tears trickling down her cheeks. She'd heard everything Dylan had said. How was it possible that he didn't love her, didn't want to spend the rest of his life with her? She loved him so fiercely, so completely that she wasn't sure she could survive when he left her. Once again, Maddie Delarue had played the fool. If she'd thought her heart had been broken a couple of times in the past, she'd been wrong. Her heart had only been bruised a little. But this time, it was broken. Broken beyond repair.

Fourteen

Several days later, Maddie and Dylan took the private airline shuttle-service into Houston. Maddie had chosen one of her favorite evening gowns, a spaghetti-strapped, floor-length number in shiny purple satin with a straight skirt and fitted bodice that accented her curves. To complete the outfit, she'd donned a pair of elbow-length gloves and three-inch heels, both in a dyed-to-match shade of deep lavender. She wore her hair in a French twist and accented the ensemble with diamond and amethyst earrings and bracelet. The moment he saw her, Dylan had told her she was beautiful. She didn't doubt his sincerity. Dylan didn't lie. He had always been completely honest with her. But his body lied. His body had promised her love and passion forever.

Maddie wasn't sure how she would get through this night—her last night with Dylan. He'd already made arrangements to fly back to Dallas tomorrow and was having his repaired Porsche sent on to him later. He had told her he wanted tonight to be special, a night they would both remember years from now. She had forced a smile and pretended that he wasn't ripping her heart to shreds with every word he spoke.

When they arrived in Houston, a limousine whisked them downtown. Inside the limo, they were cocooned in their own little world, with romantic classical music, vintage champagne, caviar, a single peach rose tied with a sheer white ribbon. And Dylan, smiling, attentive, touching her cheek lightly, caressing her bare shoulders. All the while she had to pretend that she was enjoying every moment, appreciating his thoughtfulness.

"You're awfully quiet this evening," he said.

"Am I?" She shrugged. "I suppose I'm simply overwhelmed by everything you've done. You've created the perfect date."

"I aim to please." He leaned over and brushed her lips with his.

She wanted to grab him and hold him and beg him not to leave her. But she'd never in a million years beg any man, not even Dylan Bridges. Obviously he didn't love her and didn't want to stay with her. She'd fooled herself into believing that great sex meant love. For her maybe, but not for Dylan.

"So, how well do you know Susan Wainwright?" Dylan asked.

"Susan? As well as I know most of the Wainwrights, although Susan is a few years younger than I am. I always liked her. And I envied her being tall and thin."

Dylan draped his arm around Maddie's shoulder and smiled as his gaze skimmed over her from head to toe. "Honey, you have no reason to envy another woman her figure. You've got the kind of body men dream about from the time they go through puberty until they're put six feet under."

How did he expect her to react to such a fabulous compliment? All the sweet talk and flattery in the world was a poor substitute for what Maddie really wanted: Dylan's love, now and forever.

Maddie forced herself to smile. Dear God, couldn't Dylan see through her brave pretense?

"You know, I hated the ballet when I was a teenager and my dad used to take me," Dylan said. "I didn't fully appreciate the art form until about six years ago, when I dated a lady who was mad about ballet."

"Oh, is that right?" Maddie kept her false smile firmly in place.

"You'd like Babs. You two have quite a lot in common. She's a redhead who looks good in purple. She loves the ballet and the opera and has exquisite taste."

"Sounds like a lovely person."

"She is."

"I suppose you'll be seeing Babs when you go back to Dallas."

"Probably. She's married to one of my business partners and the mother of my godson."

Maddie sighed and something inside her released.

Relief? Rage? "If she was so wonderful, it's a shame your partner stole her away from you."

"It didn't happen that way." Dylan nuzzled Maddie's neck. "Babs and I were never more than good friends."

"The way you and I are good friends," Maddie said.

Dylan lifted his hand, grasped her chin and forced her to look directly at him. "No, honey, not friends and lovers. Babs and I were only friends. And for your information, what I've had with you is not like anything I've ever had with another woman."

Then why are you leaving me? she wanted to shout. If what we've shared is so unique, so special, how can you walk away so easily?

"Yes, so you've said before." Maddie pulled his hand away from her face, but held it for several minutes.

"We should make plans for you to come for a visit to Dallas sometime," he said. "I wouldn't want us to lose touch."

"No, I...I wouldn't want that either."

"Great. Then we're in agreement." He lifted her hand to his lips and kissed it.

Later that evening, Maddie found herself trying very hard to concentrate on the performance, to allow the on-stage melodrama to overshadow her personal misery. *Madame Butterfly* was one of her favorite ballets as well as one of her favorite operas. The two-act drama, danced to the music of Puccini's famous opera, told the heartbreaking tale of a beautiful young geisha betrayed by a callous U.S. Navy officer at the turn of the nineteenth century.

Occasionally she caught a glimpse in her peripheral vision of Dylan glancing at her, and from time to time he'd reach over and squeeze her hand. He seemed the same as he'd been a day ago, a week ago, yet how could he be the same when he knew this was their last night together? But ending their relationship—did they even have a true relationship?—had been his decision, not hers. He wasn't dying inside; his heart wasn't bleeding.

Enough of this self-pity, Maddie told herself. You've recovered from a broken heart before; you can do it again. It'll just take a little longer this time because this time you really are in love. This wasn't a teenage infatuation with a football hero or a whirlwind royal romance. Dylan is your soul mate. You've known that, in your heart, since you were sixteen.

Too bad he doesn't know it!

Dylan leaned over and whispered, "Susan Wainwright is brilliant as Cio-Cio-San, isn't she?"

"Yes, she is. Absolutely brilliant." Thank God, she'd seen Susan perform on other occasions and could truthfully testify that she was a gifted ballerina.

Suddenly, right in the middle of the enthralling wedding night pas de deux, Susan Wainwright collapsed on stage. The entire audience gasped in unison.

The curtain closed and loud murmurs rose throughout the theater.

"Oh, mercy." Maddie clutched Dylan's hand. "I know there's no way to get backstage, but I wish that somehow we could find out what happened and how Susan is."

Several minutes ticked by before the announcement was made that Ms. Wainwright was resting comfortably in her dressing room and would be taken to the hospital shortly, but that she was conscious and alert. A substitute performer would temporarily replace Ms. Wainwright.

"I'd like to leave," Maddie said.

"Would you like to see if we can find out more about Susan?"

Maddie shook her head. "I'm sure they've called her family. And if they're taking her to the hospital, we might just get in the way. I'm so relieved that she's at least conscious. I'd heard that she had health problems—just Mission Creek rumors, of course."

Dylan led Maddie out of the theater to their waiting limousine. Once inside, he pulled a shivering Maddie into his arms. She clung to him.

"Oh, Dylan, when she collapsed that way, I thought she was dead. I don't know why, but I sensed that she'd had a heart attack. People can die instantly, you know. They're here with us one minute and the next they're gone." Maddie eased away just enough to look into his eyes. "Just like your father...and my father."

"And my mother," Dylan said. Dear God, Maddie was right. Life was all too brief and therefore precious. Not to be wasted.

"Susan is younger than I am. What if she... Oh, Dylan." Maddie wept on his shoulder.

Dylan held her, caressing her back, pressing his cheek against hers. Younger than I am. Younger than I am. Maddie's words echoed inside his mind. What if it had been Maddie who had collapsed, struck down in her prime? What if instead of a lovely and talented woman he barely knew, Maddie was the one being rushed to the hospital right now?

The thought of losing Maddie was unbearable. Why the hell hadn't he realized the fact that he loved Maddie Delarue as deeply and completely as it was humanly possible to love? Why had he fooled himself into thinking that they were friends and lovers and nothing more? Maddie was his other half, the one woman on earth meant for him. They fit together perfectly—in and out of bed.

But what if she doesn't love you? he asked himself. What if she doesn't trust you enough to marry you? Then you'll have to find a way to earn her trust. Do whatever the hell you have to do. And what about all those people who'll say you married Maddie to get your hands on Delarue, Inc.? To hell with them! What did he care what people thought?

You've gotten Maddie in trouble more than once. How can you be so sure you won't do it again? He couldn't be sure. After all, he was only human. He'd made his share of mistakes and he'd probably make a few more in the future. And what about trusting Maddie? Dammit, man, the woman possesses a talent for unswerving loyalty. She'd never desert you, never turn her back on you.

Dylan kissed Maddie until neither of them could breathe, and after they came up for air, he kissed her again. When they arrived at the airport, he was still kissing her.

He wanted to take this woman home—home to bed. And he intended to make lovc to her for the rest of the night. Tomorrow, when she woke in his arms, he would thank God again for Maddie's life.

By the way Dylan had been acting, Maddie suspected that he had been as shaken by Susan Wainwright's collapse on stage as she had been. He seemed to need to reaffirm the fact that they were both alive and well. Maddie understood; she felt the same.

The minute they arrived at her condo, they began stripping off their clothes in a frenzied rush to the bedroom. Somehow, right now, it didn't seem to matter that this would be their last night together, that tomorrow Dylan was going back to Dallas. He was with her now, here, this moment. And he was kissing her and touching her and wanting her as desperately as she wanted him. Life was fleeting. An ephemeral dance that ended all too soon. Reach out and grab happiness while you can, she told herself.

They landed together in the middle of her bed. Naked and panting, hungry for life and love and carnal pleasure, Maddie and Dylan mated with pure, primitive passion. Sweet preliminaries didn't matter. Protection wasn't even considered. Promises of commitment never came to mind. And foreplay became the act itself, the desire to physically bond greater than all other needs. Lifting her hips to meet him, Dylan entered her body with a powerful thrust, embedding himself inside her, becoming one being with her. Maddie moaned with the absolute rightness of their joining. The feel of him inside her was an indescribable pleasure. The intensity of their lovemaking brought them to strong, quick, simultaneous climaxes.

They lay together, embracing and kissing, as the aftershocks rippled through their bodies. Neither said a word. Words were unnecessary at that moment.

They slept awhile, then woke to make love again. Slower, more tenderly, but no less passionate. They turned and tumbled, panted and sighed. He took the dominant position at first, only to surrender to her command later. They gave and took, thinking of themselves and thinking of each other, until Maddie didn't know where she left off and where Dylan began. There was no I; there was no he. Only we. Nonexistent alone; everything together.

Maddie woke around nine o'clock and found herself all alone in her big bed. The rumpled covers, half on the floor, the other half hanging to the side of the bed, and the strong smell of sex and Dylan's unique scent were the only evidence that he had spent the night with her. Her body ached as she got out of bed and retrieved a silk robe from her closet. Sweet aches, the results of torrid lovemaking. She moved from room to room, searching for her lover. The condo was empty.

Where was Thelma? Maddie wondered, then remembered it was Saturday morning. Thelma didn't work on weekends.

Had Dylan slipped away while she slept, leaving her without saying goodbye, making sure she didn't plead with him to stay? Would he call her later? Would he drop by on his way out of town? Or was it over; was this the end of their love affair?

She would cry if she weren't suddenly so numb. Blessedly numb, as if she'd received a shot of Novocain strong enough to deaden her inside and out. She moved as if in a trance, returning to her bedroom and entering her private bath. She showered, washed and dried her hair, then dressed in casual khaki slacks and a coral knit top. Later in the kitchen, she prepared coffee and toast before reading the morning paper and telephoning Archy Wainwright to ask about Susan. Maddie was told that Susan was in the hospital for observation and tests. Either that was all the Wainwright patriarch knew or all he wanted to tell anyone outside the family.

By eleven o'clock she decided that if she didn't get out of her condo, she would go mad. Maybe she should drive by 1010 Royal Avenue and see if Dylan's rental car was still there. His plane wasn't supposed to leave until nearly four this afternoon, so he had to be somewhere. She could stop by in town and pick up some sort of farewell gift, she told herself. Any excuse to see him one more time.

You're pitiful! Listen to yourself. Why are you so desperate to hang on to a man who doesn't want you? Because I love him! That's why.

Just as Maddie picked up her purse and car keys and headed out, someone rang the doorbell. Maddie dumped her keys and purse in the velvet Louis XIV chair in the foyer, then glanced through the peephole. There stood Dylan. With her heart beating wildly, she slung open the door.

"Hey, Red, you're going to have to give me a key to this place," he said as he walked in, grabbed her around the waist and lifted her off her feet. "If I'm going to live here, I need access to the place so I won't have to keep ringing the doorbell to get in."

"Dylan? What are you— Where did you go? I thought you'd— Did you say you're going to live here?"

He planted a kiss on her nose, then set her back on her feet. "Yeah, I guess so. Unless you want to move into my dad's house. It's a little cramped and old-fashioned for your style, but—''

Maddie reached up and grabbed his face between her hands. ''What are you talking about? You're not making any sense.''

''I'm not?'' He laughed. ''I guess I am sort of putting the cart before the horse. I haven't even asked you, have I? You might say no.'' He grinned. ''Nah, you won't say no, will you? You do love me, don't you, Maddie? I mean really, honest-to-goodness love me?''

She released her hold on him and stepped back, putting several feet between them. ''Dylan, you're confusing me.''

''Yeah, I know the feeling. I've been confused about us, too. But last night everything became crystal clear. Nothing matters, not your money, not my past history, nothing. All that matters is you and me and our being together. Right?''

Maddie stared at him in total shock.

''Look, Red, I think the first thing we need to do is get your lawyers to draw up an ironclad prenuptial agreement. That way there'll be no question of me marrying you for your money or taking charge of Delarue, Inc.''

''Prenuptial agreement?''

''Yeah, honey, aren't you listening to me?''

''Dylan, are you asking me to marry you?''

He burst into laughter, then pulled her into his arms.

"God, I knew I'd screw this up. Do you want me to get down on one knee?"

"No, I want you to explain where you've been, what's happened to you and—"

He kissed her. Quick and hard. "I've been to the bank. If they weren't open till noon on Saturday, I'd have had to wait until Monday to get this." He stuck his hand in his pants pocket and pulled out a small velvet pouch, opened it and dumped the contents into his hand. Leda Bridges' one-carat solitaire engagement ring and gold wedding band lay in the center of Dylan's palm. He stuck the solitaire on the tip of his pinkie, then put the band back in the pouch. "We'll save that until later."

Maddie stared at the shimmering diamond ring as Dylan removed it from his pinkie and held it out to her. "Maddie, I love you. You have no idea how much I love you. Hell, I had no idea how much I loved you until last night."

While she gazed at the ring, her eyes misting with tears as she absorbed his declaration of love, Dylan grabbed her hand, lifted it and slipped the ring on the third finger of her left hand. A perfect fit. This ring was meant to be hers. "Will you marry me?"

"Yes."

"Yes?"

She nodded. "Yes."

He followed her line of vision straight to the ring. "I know it's only a one-carat diamond. I could afford something bigger, more expensive, but this was my mother's and—"

"I love this ring," she told him. "Almost as much as I love you."

"It's about time you got around to telling me you love me."

She gazed up at him, but could barely see him through the shower of tears. "I think I've loved you forever. Well, at least since I was sixteen."

"Yeah, I guess I've loved you ever since way back then, too. I don't know why it's taken me so damn long to figure it out. I knew I wanted you. I knew you were the best thing that ever happened to me. And I knew sex between us was great." He kissed her again. "You know, Red, you're marrying a real dope."

"We're getting married. You and me. A wedding. A honeymoon. A life together."

"Yeah, and we're going to make it a happily-ever-after life. I'm making you that promise and it's one I intend to keep."

Happiness burst inside Maddie, filling her completely. She closed her eyes and sighed. "I want babies. Your babies."

"Hey, you could be pregnant now, you know. We did kind of get a head start on the honeymoon."

"Would you mind if I am pregnant?"

"I'd kind of like to have you all to myself for a while, but if you are, I won't mind too much."

Maddie giggled as she snuggled closer, stood on

tiptoe and spoke with her lips lightly brushing his, "Tell me again."

"Tell you what?"

"That you love me."

"Oh, sweet Maddie, I'm going to be telling you I love you every day for at least the next fifty years."

"Only once a day?"

"Twice a day. Ten times a day. As many times as you want to hear it."

"Say it."

"I love you, Maddie Delarue. I love you, I love you, I love you."

Dylan swept her off her feet and up into his arms. Just as he headed for the bedroom, the doorbell chimed. "Damn. Let's ignore it."

The doorbell rang again and again.

"Whoever it is seems persistent. They probably won't go away."

A familiar voice called, "Maddie, I know you're home, so you might as well open the door and let me in. I am not leaving until I speak to you."

Maddie groaned. "It's my mother."

With Maddie still in his arms, Dylan waltzed back into the foyer, reached out and opened the front door.

"Come right in, Nadine," Dylan said. "Or would you rather I call you Mother Delarue?"

"Just what's going on here?" Nadine asked. "Have the two of you been drinking? You act as if you're drunk."

"We're drunk on love," Dylan told her.

Nadine gasped. "You were carrying my daughter off to the bedroom, weren't you? And it's not even noon yet."

"Mother, Dylan and I have something to tell you."

"There's nothing I want to hear about you and Mr. Bridges," Nadine said.

Dylan readjusted Maddie in his arms; she tightened her hold around his neck. "You really should start calling me Dylan. After all, it's going to look odd to your friends if you refer to your son-in-law as Mr. Bridges."

"My son-in— My God, Maddie, are you planning to marry this man?"

"Yes, Mother, I am. And as soon as possible. I might already be pregnant, so you'd better start planning the wedding today. Feel free to make it as extravagant as you'd like and spend a million dollars if you want to. I don't care. All I want is to become Dylan's wife."

"Pregnant?" Nadine's mouth fell open and her eyes rounded in surprise. "You're...you're pregnant?"

"If she isn't, she will be soon," Dylan said. "Now, Mother Delarue, if you don't mind, Maddie and I have some pre-wedding plans of our own to make."

"You're asking me to leave?" Nadine glared at Dylan.

"Only for now. You'll always be welcome in our

home,'' he told her. ''After all, we're counting on you to be our number-one baby-sitter.''

''I—I don't know what to say.'' Nadine looked directly at Maddie.

''Say that you're happy for me,'' Maddie suggested.

Nadine glanced back at Dylan. ''I'll expect to play a major role in my grandchildren's lives.''

''Of course,'' Dylan said. ''All children need a special grandmother to spoil them rotten.''

Nadine smiled. ''Congratulations, young man. She's much too good for you, you know.''

''Yes, ma'am, I know.''

''Maddie, if you love him, then I'm happy for you. He's not quite what I wanted, but I suppose he'll do. He does seem to genuinely care about you and...he certainly knows how to win over his mother-in-law.'' Nadine pointed her finger at Dylan. ''If you ever hurt her or disappoint her or cause her one moment of unhappiness, you'll have to answer to me.''

''Oh, Mother, how sweet of you to—''

''I'm leaving now.'' Nadine crossed the threshold, then glanced back over her shoulder. ''I expect y'all at my house for dinner tonight. Seven sharp. We have a wedding to plan.''

''We'll be there,'' Maddie said.

Nadine waved a dismissal gesture. ''Go on with what you were doing before I interrupted you.''

The minute his future mother-in-law left, Dylan

laughed. ''That's the first time a girl's mother ever gave me permission to make love to her.''

''That's the first time a girl's mother wanted you to get her pregnant.''

''Well, let's not disappoint Grandma.''

Dylan carried Maddie to bed and with every touch, every kiss, every whispered endearment, he pledged his love and devotion. And two lonely souls united, having finally found not only true love, but complete trust.

* * * * *

Don't miss the next story from
Silhouette's
LONE STAR COUNTRY CLUB:

HEARTBREAKER
by Laurie Paige
Available September 2002

Turn the page for an excerpt from this exciting romance...!

One

The twin engines of Michael O'Day's new plane purred steadily as he buzzed the field in preparation for landing at Mission Ridge, a ''fly-in, fly-out'' community on the outskirts of Mission Creek, Texas. No planes were on the runway, and none was heading in for a landing, other than his.

From the air, he could pick out the home he'd purchased last year. It was a big house for a bachelor, not yet completely furnished, but he was pleased with it.

With the private airstrip at his door and the Lone Star Country Club golf links nearby, he could indulge his two favorite pastimes: golfing and flying. He planned to retire here.

But not anytime soon. At thirty-four, he had a ways to go before riding off into the sunset. However, with the new, faster plane, it would be a piece of cake to fly the 250 miles back and forth to Houston where he had a penthouse and an office. As a heart surgeon, he kept a busy schedule.

He set the nimble four-passenger plane down on the tarmac and taxied off the runway, heading for his hangar at the back of his two-acre lot. Instead of pushing the plane inside when he arrived, he left it on the apron. He was running late for lunch with his friend and golfing buddy, Flynt Carson. He'd take care of the aircraft later.

He dashed across the back lawn and into the garage attached to the house, hitting the button to open the garage door as he did. Inside he swung his legs over the car door and into the seat of the low-slung convertible he kept at Mission Ridge.

Checking his watch, he grimaced and turned the ignition key. He drove out of the garage, hit the button to lower the door behind him, glanced to his left and, seeing no traffic, gunned the engine.

And immediately threw on the brakes.

The car came to a screeching halt about six inches from a tall, lithe beauty who was standing in the middle of the street. She turned flashing green eyes on him.

"You baboon!" she said in an angry, albeit melodious voice. "You shouldn't be allowed behind the wheel, driving like a maniac down a residential street."

"Well, honey," he drawled, amused and irritated by her lofty manner, "I didn't expect some female..." Translation: some ditz "...to be sashaying down the middle of the street."

"I am not sashaying down the middle of the street. I happen to be crossing it."

He studied her, then glanced across the street and back to her. "You might not know it," he mentioned in a helpful, philosophical tone, "but the shortest distance between two points is a straight line. Going straight across the street gets you to the other side faster than ambling across at an oblique angle. It could save you from getting run over."

"And watching where you're going could save you from killing someone and getting thrown in jail."

"A point well taken," he agreed, unable to kill the grin. In blue slacks and a knit top that outlined her to perfection, she was very easy on the eye. Besides which, he'd always been attracted to women with fire.

He watched her march on across the street, her head high, her light brown hair swinging about her shoulders. He'd never seen anyone move the way she did, with the grace and dignity of a fairy princess. And the righteous anger of a tent evangelist.

A name came to him. Susan Wainwright.

He'd never met her, but he'd seen her a few times on stage. She was a lead ballerina with the Houston Ballet.

Her sister had recently wed Matt Carson. A surprising affair, considering the Carsons and Wainwrights had been feuding for nearly as long as the Hatfields and McCoys. But Michael recalled hearing a rumor of a truce for the wedding.

Watching the delectable sway of her hips, he formed a new appreciation for a dancer's grace of movement. To his surprise, a vision came to mind—him and her in a wide bed, those long legs wrapped around him—

Whoa!

Shaking his head, he forced those thoughts aside. "Hey," he called. "You need a ride somewhere?"

She gave him a drop-dead glance. "No, thanks. Someone is picking me up."

A fleeting notion indicated he'd like the someone to be him. Forget it, he advised. That little gal was a heartbreaker from the get-go. Besides, he wasn't looking for any lengthy entanglement. His life was fine just as it was.

Grinning at himself, he eased down on the pedal and left the enticing and oh-so-haughty beauty behind.